UNDINE

By

FRIEDRICH
DE LA MOTTE FOUQUÉ

WITH INTRODUCTORY ESSAYS
BY GEORGE MACDONALD
AND LAFCADIO HEARN

First published in 1811

Read & Co.

Copyright © 2020 Read & Co. Books

This edition is published by Read & Co. Books,
an imprint of Read & Co.

This book is copyright and may not be reproduced or copied in any
way without the express permission of the publisher in writing.

British Library Cataloguing-in-Publication Data
A catalogue record for this book is available
from the British Library.

Read & Co. is part of Read Books Ltd.
For more information visit
www.readandcobooks.co.uk

TO UNDINE

Undine! thou fair and lovely sprite,
　Since first from out an ancient lay
I saw gleam forth thy fitful light,
　How hast thou sung my cares away!

How hast thou nestled next my heart,
And gently offered to impart
　Thy sorrows to my listening ear,
Like a half-shy, half-trusting child,
The while my lute, in wood-notes wild,
　Thine accents echoed far and near!
Then many a youth I won to muse
　With love on thy mysterious ways,
With many a fair one to peruse
　The legend of thy wondrous days.

And now both dame and youth would fain
List to my tale yet once again;
　Nay, sweet Undine, be not afraid!
Enter their halls with footsteps light,
Greet courteously each noble knight,
　But fondly every German maid.

And should they ask concerning me,
　Oh, say, "He is a cavalier,
Who truly serves and valiantly,
In tourney and festivity,
　With lute and sword, each lady fair!"

CONTENTS

THE
FANTASTIC
IMAGINATION

By George Macdonald

That we have in English no word corresponding to the German *Mährchen*, drives us to use the word *Fairytale*, regardless of the fact that the tale may have nothing to do with any sort of fairy. The old use of the word *Fairy*, by Spenser at least, might, however, well be adduced, were justification or excuse necessary where *need must*.

Were I asked, what is a fairytale? I should reply, *Read Undine: that is a fairytale; then read this and that as well, and you will see what is a fairytale*. Were I further begged to describe the *fairytale*, or define what it is, I would make answer, that I should as soon think of describing the abstract human face, or stating what must go to constitute a human being. A fairytale is just a fairytale, as a face is just a face; and of all fairytales I know, I think *Undine* the most beautiful.

Many a man, however, who would not attempt to define *a man*, might venture to say something as to what a man ought to be: even so much I will not in this place venture with regard to the fairytale, for my long past work in that kind might but poorly instance or illustrate my now more matured judgment. I will but say some things helpful to the reading, in right-minded fashion, of such fairytales as I would wish to write, or care to read.

Some thinkers would feel sorely hampered if at liberty to use no forms but such as existed in nature, or to invent nothing save in accordance with the laws of the world of the senses;

but it must not therefore be imagined that they desire escape from the region of law. Nothing lawless can show the least reason why it should exist, or could at best have more than an appearance of life.

The natural world has its laws, and no man must interfere with them in the way of presentment any more than in the way of use; but they themselves may suggest laws of other kinds, and man may, if he pleases, invent a little world of his own, with its own laws; for there is that in him which delights in calling up new forms—which is the nearest, perhaps, he can come to creation. When such forms are new embodiments of old truths, we call them products of the Imagination; when they are mere inventions, however lovely, I should call them the work of the Fancy: in either case, Law has been diligently at work.

His world once invented, the highest law that comes next into play is, that there shall be harmony between the laws by which the new world has begun to exist; and in the process of his creation, the inventor must hold by those laws. The moment he forgets one of them, he makes the story, by its own postulates, incredible. To be able to live a moment in an imagined world, we must see the laws of its existence obeyed. Those broken, we fall out of it. The imagination in us, whose exercise is essential to the most temporary submission to the imagination of another, immediately, with the disappearance, of Law, ceases to act. Suppose the gracious creatures of some childlike region of Fairyland talking either cockney or Gascon! Would not the tale, however lovelily begun, sink at once to the level of the Burlesque—of all forms of literature the least worthy? A man's inventions may be stupid or clever, but if he do not hold by the laws of them, or if he make one law jar with another, he contradicts himself as an inventor, he is no artist. He does not rightly consort his instruments, or he tunes them in different keys. The mind of man is the product of live Law; it thinks by law, it dwells in the midst of law, it gathers from law its growth; with law, therefore, can it alone work to any result.

Inharmonious, unconsorting ideas will come to a man, but if he try to use one of such, his work will grow dull, and he will drop it from mere lack of interest. Law is the soil in which alone beauty will grow; beauty is the only stuff in which Truth can be clothed; and you may, if you will, call Imagination the tailor that cuts her garments to fit her, and Fancy his journeyman that puts the pieces of them together, or perhaps at most embroiders their button-holes. Obeying law, the maker works like his creator; not obeying law, he is such a fool as heaps a pile of stones and calls it a church.

In the moral world it is different: there a man may clothe in new forms, and for this employ his imagination freely, but he must invent nothing. He may not, for any purpose, turn its laws upside down. He must not meddle with the relations of live souls. The laws of the spirit of man must hold, alike in this world and in any world he may invent. It were no offence to suppose a world in which everything repelled instead of attracted the things around it; it would be wicked to write a tale representing a man it called good as always doing bad things, or a man it called bad as always doing good things: the notion itself is absolutely lawless. In physical things a man may invent; in moral things he must obey—and take their laws with him into his invented world as well.

"You write as if a fairytale were a thing of importance: must it have a meaning?"

It cannot help having some meaning; if it have proportion and harmony it has vitality, and vitality is truth. The beauty may be plainer in it than the truth, but without the truth the beauty could not be, and the fairytale would give no delight. Everyone, however, who feels the story, will read its meaning after his own nature and development: one man will read one meaning in it, another will read another.

"If so, how am I to assure myself that I am not reading my own meaning into it, but yours out of it?"

Why should you be so assured? It may be better that you

should read your meaning into it. That may be a higher operation of your intellect than the mere reading of mine out of it: your meaning may be superior to mine.

"Suppose my child ask me what the fairytale means, what am I to say?"

If you do not know what it means, what is easier than to say so? If you do see a meaning in it, there it is for you to give him. A genuine work of art must mean many things; the truer its art, the more things it will mean. If my drawing, on the other hand, is so far from being a work of art that it needs THIS IS A HORSE written under it, what can it matter that neither you nor your child should know what it means? It is there not so much to convey a meaning as to wake a meaning. If it do not even wake an interest, throw it aside. A meaning may be there, but it is not for you. If, again, you do not know a horse when you see it, the name written under it will not serve you much. At all events, the business of the painter is not to teach zoology.

But indeed your children are not likely to trouble you about the meaning. They find what they are capable of finding, and more would be too much. For my part, I do not write for children, but for the childlike, whether of five, or fifty, or seventy-five.

A fairytale is not an allegory. There may be allegory in it, but it is not an allegory. He must be an artist indeed who can, in any mode, produce a strict allegory that is not a weariness to the spirit. An allegory must be Mastery or Moorditch.

A fairytale, like a butterfly or a bee, helps itself on all sides, sips at every wholesome flower, and spoils not one. The true fairytale is, to my mind, very like the sonata. We all know that a sonata means something; and where there is the faculty of talking with suitable vagueness, and choosing metaphor sufficiently loose, mind may approach mind, in the interpretation of a sonata, with the result of a more or less contenting consciousness of sympathy. But if two or three men sat down to write each what the sonata meant to him, what approximation to definite idea would be the result? Little enough—and that little more than needful. We should find it had roused related, if not identical, feelings, but probably not one common thought. Has the sonata therefore failed? Had it undertaken to convey, or ought it to be expected to impart anything defined, anything notionally recognizable?

"But words are not music; words at least are meant and fitted to carry a precise meaning!"

It is very seldom indeed that they carry the exact meaning of any user of them! And if they can be so used as to convey definite meaning, it does not follow that they ought never to carry anything else. Words are live things that may be variously employed to various ends. They can convey a scientific fact, or throw a shadow of her child's dream on the heart of a mother. They are things to put together like the pieces of a dissected map, or to arrange like the notes on a stave. Is the music in them to go for nothing? It can hardly help the definiteness of a meaning: is it therefore to be disregarded? They have length, and breadth, and outline: have they nothing to do with depth? Have they only to describe, never to impress? Has nothing any claim to their use but the definite? The cause of a child's tears may be altogether undefinable: has the mother therefore no antidote for his vague misery? That may be strong in colour which has no evident outline. A fairytale, a sonata, a gathering storm, a limitless night, seizes you and sweeps you away: do you begin at once to wrestle with it and ask whence its power over you, whither it is carrying you? The law of each is in the mind of its composer; that law makes one man feel this way, another man feel that way. To one the sonata is a world of odour and beauty, to another of soothing only and sweetness. To one, the cloudy rendezvous is a wild dance, with a terror at its heart; to another, a majestic march of heavenly hosts, with Truth in their centre pointing their course, but as yet restraining her voice. The greatest forces lie in the region of the uncomprehended.

I will go farther.—The best thing you can do for your fellow, next to rousing his conscience, is—not to give him things to

11

think about, but to wake things up that are in him; or say, to make him think things for himself. The best Nature does for us is to work in us such moods in which thoughts of high import arise. Does any aspect of Nature wake but one thought? Does she ever suggest only one definite thing? Does she make any two men in the same place at the same moment think the same thing? Is she therefore a failure, because she is not definite? Is it nothing that she rouses the something deeper than the understanding—the power that underlies thoughts? Does she not set feeling, and so thinking at work? Would it be better that she did this after one fashion and not after many fashions? Nature is mood-engendering, thought-provoking: such ought the sonata, such ought the fairytale to be.

"But a man may then imagine in your work what he pleases, what you never meant!"

Not what he pleases, but what he can. If he be not a true man, he will draw evil out of the best; we need not mind how he treats any work of art! If he be a true man, he will imagine true things; what matter whether I meant them or not? They are there none the less that I cannot claim putting them there! One difference between God's work and man's is, that, while God's work cannot mean more than he meant, man's must mean more than he meant. For in everything that God has made, there is layer upon layer of ascending significance; also he expresses the same thought in higher and higher kinds of that thought: it is God's things, his embodied thoughts, which alone a man has to use, modified and adapted to his own purposes, for the expression of his thoughts; therefore he cannot help his words and figures falling into such combinations in the mind of another as he had himself not foreseen, so many are the thoughts allied to every other thought, so many are the relations involved in every figure, so many the facts hinted in every symbol. A man may well himself discover truth in what he wrote; for he was dealing all the time with things that came from thoughts beyond his own.

"But surely you would explain your idea to one who asked you?"

I say again, if I cannot draw a horse, I will not write THIS IS A HORSE under what I foolishly meant for one. Any key to a work of imagination would be nearly, if not quite, as absurd. The tale is there, not to hide, but to show: if it show nothing at your window, do not open your door to it; leave it out in the cold. To ask me to explain, is to say, "Roses! Boil them, or we won't have them!" My tales may not be roses, but I will not boil them.

So long as I think my dog can bark, I will not sit up to bark for him.

If a writer's aim be logical conviction, he must spare no logical pains, not merely to be understood, but to escape being misunderstood; where his object is to move by suggestion, to cause to imagine, then let him assail the soul of his reader as the wind assails an aeolian harp. If there be music in my reader, I would gladly wake it. Let fairytale of mine go for a firefly that now flashes, now is dark, but may flash again. Caught in a hand which does not love its kind, it will turn to an insignificant, ugly thing, that can neither flash nor fly.

The best way with music, I imagine, is not to bring the forces of our intellect to bear upon it, but to be still and let it work on that part of us for whose sake it exists. We spoil countless precious things by intellectual greed. He who will be a man, and will not be a child, must—he cannot help himself—become a little man, that is, a dwarf. He will, however, need no consolation, for he is sure to think himself a very large creature indeed.

If any strain of my "broken music" make a child's eyes flash, or his mother's grow for a moment dim, my labour will not have been in vain.

A Chapter from
A Dish of Orts, 1893

THE VALUE OF THE
SUPERNATURAL IN FICTION

By Lafcadio Hearn

1915

The subject of this lecture is much more serious than may appear to you from this title. Young men of your age are not likely to believe in ghosts, nor inclined to consider the subject as worthy of attention. The first things necessary to understand are the philosophical and literary relations of the topic. Let me tell you that it would be a mistake to suppose that the stories of the supernatural have had their day in fine literature. On the contrary, wherever fine literature is being produced, either in poetry or in prose, you will find the supernatural element very much alive. Scientific knowledge has not at all diminished the pleasure of mankind in this field of imagination, though it may have considerably changed the methods of treatment. The success of writers of to-day like Maeterlinck is chiefly explained by their skill in the treatment of the ghostly, and of subjects related to supernatural fear. But without citing other living writers, let me observe that there is scarcely any really great author in European literature, old or new, who has not distinguished himself in the treatment of the supernatural. In English literature, I believe there is no exception—even from the time of the Anglo-Saxon poets to Shakespeare, and from Shakespeare to our own day. And this introduces us to the consideration of a general and remarkable fact, a fact that I do not remember to have seen in any books, but which is of very great philosophical importance; there is something ghostly in all great art, whether of literature, music, sculpture, or architecture.

But now let me speak to you about this word "ghostly"; it is a much bigger word, perhaps, than some of you imagine. The old English had no other word for "spiritual" or "supernatural"— which two terms you know, are not English but Latin. Everything that religion to-day calls divine, holy, miraculous, was sufficiently explained for the old Anglo-Saxons by the term ghostly. They spoke of a man's ghost, instead of speaking of his spirit or soul; and everything relating to religious knowledge they called ghostly. In the modern formula of the Catholic confession, which has remained almost unchanged for nearly two thousand years, you will find that the priest is always called a "ghostly" father—which means that his business is to take care of the ghosts or souls of men as a father does. In addressing the priest, the penitent really calls him "Father of my ghost." You will see, therefore, that a very large meaning really attaches to the adjective. It means everything relating to the supernatural. It means to the Christian even God himself, for the Giver of Life is always called in English the Holy Ghost.

Accepting the evolutional philosophy which teaches that the modern idea of God as held by western nations is really but a development from the primitive belief in a shadow-soul, the term ghost in its reference to the supreme being certainly could not be found fault with. On the contrary, there is a weirdness about this use of the word which adds greatly to its solemnity. But whatever belief we have, or have not, as regards religious creeds, one thing that modern science has done for us, is to prove beyond all question that everything which we used to consider material and solid is essentially ghostly, as is any ghost. If we do not believe in old-fashioned stories and theories about ghosts, we are nevertheless obliged to recognise to-day that we are ghosts of ourselves—and utterly incomprehensible. The mystery of the universe is now weighing upon us, becoming heavier and heavier, more and more awful, as our knowledge expands, and it is especially a ghostly mystery. All great art reminds us in some way of this universal riddle; that is why I say that all great art has something ghostly in it. It touches something within us which relates to infinity. When you read a very great thought, when you see a wonderful picture or statue or building, and when you hear certain kinds of music, you feel a thrill in the heart and mind much like the thrill which in all times men felt when they thought they saw a ghost or a god. Only the modern thrill is incomparably larger and longer and deeper. And this is why, in spite of all knowledge, the world still finds pleasure in the literature of the supernatural, and will continue to find pleasure in it for hundreds of years to come. The ghostly represents always some shadow of truth, and no amount of disbelief in what used to be called ghosts can ever diminish human interest in what relates to that truth.

So you will see that the subject is not altogether trifling. Certainly it is of very great moment in relation to great literature. The poet or the story-teller who can not give the reader a little ghostly pleasure at times never can be either a really great writer or a great thinker. I have already said that I know of no exception to this rule in the whole of English literature. Take, for instance, Macaulay, the most practical, hard-headed, logical writer of the century, the last man in whom you would expect to find the least trace of superstition. Had you read only certain of his essays, you would scarcely think him capable of touching the chords of the supernatural. But he has done this in a masterly way in several of the "Lays of Ancient Rome" —for example, in speaking of the apparition of the Twin Brethren at the battle of Lake Regillus, and of Tarquin haunted by the phantom of his victim Lucretia. Both of these passages give the ghostly thrill in a strong way; and there is a fainter thrill of the same sort to be experienced from the reading of parts of the "Prophecy of Capys." It is because Macaulay had this power, though using it sparingly, that his work is so great. If he had not been able to write these lines of poetry which I referred to, he could not even have made his history of England the living history that it is. A man who has no ghostly feeling can not make anything alive, not even a page of history or a page of oratory. To touch men's souls, you must know all that those souls can be made to feel by words; and to know that, you must yourself have a "ghost" in you that can be touched in the same way.

Now leaving the theoretical for the practical part of the theme, let us turn to the subject of the relation between ghosts and dreams.

No good writer—no great writer—ever makes a study of the supernatural according to anything which has been done before by other writers. This is one of those subjects upon which you can not get real help from books. It is not from books, nor from traditions, nor from legends, nor from anything of that kind that you can learn how to give your reader a ghostly thrill. I do not mean that it is of no use for you to read what has been written upon the subject, so far as mere methods of expression, mere effects of literary workmanship, are concerned. On the contrary, it is very important that you should read all you can of what is good in literature upon these subjects; you will learn from them a great deal about curious values of words, about compactness and power of sentences, about peculiarities of beliefs and of terrors relating to those beliefs. But you must never try to use another man's ideas or feelings, taken from a book, in order to make a supernatural effect. If you do, the work will never be sincere, and will never make a thrill. You must use your own ideas and feelings only, under all possible circumstances. And where are you to get these ideas and feelings from, if you do not believe in ghosts? From your dreams. Whether you believe in ghosts or not, all the artistic elements of ghostly literature exist in your dreams, and form a veritable treasury of literary material for the man that knows how to use them.

All the great effects obtained by poets and story writers, and even by religious teachers, in the treatment of supernatural fear or mystery, have been obtained, directly or indirectly, through dreams. Study any great ghost story in any literature, and you will find that no matter how surprising or unfamiliar the incidents seem, a little patient examination will prove to you that every one of them has occurred, at different times, in different combinations, in dreams of your own. They give you a thrill. But why? Because they remind you of experiences, imaginative or emotional, which you had forgotten. There can be no exception to this rule—absolutely none. I was speaking to you the other day about a short story by Bulwer Lytton, as being the best ghost story in the English language. The reason why it is the best story of this kind is simply because it represents with astonishing faithfulness the experiences of nightmare. The terror of all great stories of the supernatural is really the terror of nightmare, projected into waking consciousness. And the beauty or tenderness of other ghost stories or fairy-stories, or even of certain famous and delightful religious legends, is the tenderness and beauty of dreams of a happier kind, dreams inspired by love or hope or regret. But in all cases where the supernatural is well treated in literature, dream experience is the source of the treatment. I know that I am now speaking to an audience acquainted with literature of which I know practically nothing. But I believe that there can be no exception to these rules even in the literature of the Far East. I do not mean to say that there may not be in Chinese and in Japanese literature many ghost stories which are not derived from dream-experience. But I will say that if there are any of this kind, they are not worth reading, and can not belong to any good class of literature. I have read translations of a number of Chinese ghost stories in French, also a wonderful English translation of ghostly Chinese stories in two volumes, entitled "Strange Stories from a Chinese Studio," by Herbert Giles. These stories, translated by a great scholar, are very wonderful; but I noticed that in every successful treatment of a supernatural subject, the incidents of the story invariably correspond with the phenomena of dreams. Therefore I think that I can not be mistaken in my judgment of the matter. Such Japanese stories as I could get translations of, obeyed the same rule. The other day, in a story which I read for the first time, I was very much interested to find an exact parallel between the treatment of a supernatural idea by the Japanese author, and by the best English author of dream studies. The story was about a picture, painted upon a screen, representing a river and a landscape. In the Japanese story (perhaps it has a Chinese origin) the painter makes a sign to the screen; and a little boat begins to sail down the river, and sails out of the picture into the room, and the room becomes full of water, and the painter, or magician, or whoever he is, gets into the boat and sails away into the picture again, and disappears forever. This is exactly, in every detail, a dream story, and the excellence of it is in its truth to dream experience. The same phenomena you will find, under another form, in "Alice in Wonderland," and "Through the Looking Glass."

But to return to the point where we left off. I was saying that all successful treatment of the ghostly or the impossible must be made to correspond as much as possible with the truth of dream experience, and that Bulwer Lytton's story of the haunted house illustrates the rule. Let us now consider especially the literary value of nightmare. Nightmare, the most awful form of dream, is also one of the most peculiar. It has probably furnished all the important elements of religious and supernatural terror which are to be found in really great literature. It is a mysterious thing in itself; and scientific psychology has not yet been able to explain many facts in regard to it. We can take the phenomena of nightmare separately, one by one, and show their curious relation to various kinds of superstitious fear and supernatural belief.

The first remarkable fact in nightmare is the beginning of it. It begins with a kind of suspicion, usually. You feel afraid without knowing why. Then you have the impression that something is acting upon you from a distance — something like fascination, yet not exactly fascination, for there may be no visible fascinator.

But feeling uneasy, you wish to escape, to get away from the influence that is making you afraid. Then you find it is not easy to escape. You move with great difficulty. Presently the difficulty increases—you can not move at all. You want to cry out, and you can not; you have lost your voice. You are actually in a state of trance—seeing, hearing, feeling, but unable to move or speak. This is the beginning. It forms one of the most terrible emotions from which a man can suffer. If it continued more than a certain length of time, the mere fear might kill. Nightmare does sometimes kill, in cases where the health has been very much affected by other causes.

Of course we have nothing in ordinary waking life of such experience—the feeling of being deprived of will and held fast from a great distance by some view-less power. This is the real experience of magnetism, mesmerism; and it is the origin of certain horrible beliefs of the Middle Ages in regard to magical power. Suppose we call it supernatural mesmerism, for want of a better word. It is not true mesmerism, because in real hypnotic conditions, the patient does not feel or think or act mentally according to his own personality; he acts by the will of another. In nightmare the will is only suspended, and the personal consciousness remains; this is what makes the horror of it. So we shall call the first stage supernatural mesmerism, only with the above qualification. Now let us see how Bulwer Lytton uses this experience in his story.

A man is sitting in a chair, with a lamp on the table beside him, and is reading Macaulay's essays, when he suddenly becomes uneasy. A shadow falls upon the page. He rises, and tries to call; but he can not raise his voice above a whisper. He tries to move; and he can not stir hand or foot. The spell is already upon him. This is the first part of nightmare.

The second stage of the phenomenon, which sometimes mingles with the first stage, is the experience of terrible and unnatural appearances. There is always a darkening of the visible, sometimes a disappearance or dimming of the light.

In Bulwer Lytton's story there is a fire burning in the room, and a very bright lamp. Gradually both lamp and fire become dimmer and dimmer; at last all light completely vanishes, and the room becomes absolutely dark, except for spectral and unnatural luminosities that begin to make their appearance. This also is a very good study of dream experience. The third stage of nightmare, the final struggle, is chiefly characterised by impossible occurrences, which bring to the dreamer the extreme form of horror, while convincing him of his own impotence. For example, you try to fire a pistol or to use a steel weapon. If a pistol, the bullet will not project itself more than a few inches from the muzzle; then it drops down limply, and there is no report. If a sword or dagger, the blade becomes soft, like cotton or paper. Terrible appearances, monstrous or unnatural figures, reach out hands to touch; if human figures, they will grow to the ceiling, and bend themselves fantastically as they approach. There is one more stage, which is not often reached—the climax of the horror. That is when you are caught or touched. The touch in nightmare is a very peculiar sensation, almost like an electric shock, but unnaturally prolonged. It is not pain, but something worse than pain, an experience never felt in waking hours.

The third and fourth stages have been artistically mixed together by Bulwer Lytton. The phantom towers from floor to ceiling, vague and threatening; the man attempts to use a weapon, and at the same time receives a touch or shock that renders him absolutely powerless. He describes the feeling as resembling the sensation of some ghostly electricity. The study is exactly true to dream experience. I need not here mention this story further, since from this point a great many other elements enter into it which, though not altogether foreign to our subject, do not illustrate that subject so well as some of the stories of Poe. Poe has given us other peculiar details of nightmare-experience, such as horrible sounds. Often we hear in such dreams terrible muffled noises, as of steps coming. This you will find very well studied in the story called "The Fall of the House of Usher."

Again in these dreams inanimate objects either become alive, or suggest to us, by their motion, the hiding of some horrible life behind them— curtains, for example, doors left half open, alcoves imperfectly closed. Poe has studied these in "Eleonora" and in some other sketches.

Dreams of the terrible have beyond question had a good deal to do with the inspiration both of religious and of superstitious literature. The returning of the dead, visions of heavenly or infernal beings,—these, when well described, are almost always exact reproductions of dream-experience. But occasionally we find an element of waking fear mixed with them—for example, in one of the oldest ghost stories of the world, the story in "The Book of Job." The poet speaks of feeling intense cold, and feeling the hairs of his head stand up with fear. These experiences are absolutely true, and they belong to waking life. The sensation of cold and the sensation of horror are not sensations of dreams. They come from extraordinary terror felt in active existence, while we are awake. You will observe the very same signs of fear in a horse, a dog, or a cat—and there is reason to suppose that in these animal cases, also, supernatural fear is sometimes a cause. I have seen a dog—a brave dog, too—terribly frightened by seeing a mass of paper moved by a slight current of air. This slight wind did not reach the place where the dog was lying; he could not therefore associate the motion of the paper with a motion of the wind; he did not understand what was moving the paper; the mystery alarmed him, and the hair on his back stood up with fear. But the mingling of such sensations of waking fear with dream sensations of fear, in a story or poem, may be very effectually managed, so as to give to the story an air of reality, of actuality, which could not be obtained in any other way. A great many of our old fairy ballads and goblin stories mixed the two experiences together with the most excellent results. I should say that the fine German story of "Undine" is a good example of this kind. The sight of the faces in the water of the river, the changing of waterfalls and cataracts into ghostly people, the rising from

23

the closed well of the form of Undine herself, the rising of the flood behind her, and the way in which she "weeps her lover to death"—all this is pure dream; and it seems real because most of us have had some such experiences of fancy in our own dreams. But the other part of the story, dealing with human emotions, fears, passions—these are of waking life, and the mixture is accomplished in a most artistic way. Speaking of Undine obliges me also to speak of Undine's predecessors in mediaeval literature—the mediaeval spirits, the succubae and incubi, the sylphs and salamanders or salamandrines, the whole wonderful goblin population of water, air, forest, and fire. All the good stories about them are really dream studies. And coming down to the most romantic literature of our own day, the same thing must be said of those strange and delightful stories by Gautier, "La Morte Amoureuse," "Arria Marcella," "Le Pied de Momie." The most remarkable is perhaps "La Morte Amoureuse"; but there is in this a study of double personality, which complicates it too much for purposes of present illustration. I shall therefore speak of "Arria Marcella" instead. Some young students visit the city of Pompeii, to study the ruins and the curiosities preserved in the museum of Naples, nearby. All of them are familiar with classic literature and classic history; moreover, they are artists, able to appreciate the beauty of what they see. At the time of the eruption, which occurred nearly two thousand years ago, many people perished by being smothered under the rain of ashes; but their bodies were encased in the deposit so that the form was perfectly preserved as in a mould. Some of these moulds are to be seen in the museum mentioned; and one is the mould of the body of a beautiful young woman. The younger of the three students sees this mould, and romantically wishes that he could see and love the real person, so many centuries dead. That night, while his companions are asleep, he leaves his room and wanders into the ruined city, for the pleasure of thinking all by himself. But presently, as he turns the corner of a street, he finds that the city looks quite different from what it had appeared by

24

day; the houses seem to have grown taller; they look new, bright, clean. While he is thus wandering, suddenly the sun rises, and the streets fill with people—not the people of to-day, but the people of two thousand years ago, all dressed in the old Greek and Roman costumes. After a time a young Greek comes up to the student and speaks to him in Latin. He has learned enough Latin at the university to be able to answer, and a conversation begins, of which the result is that he is invited to the theatre of Pompeii to see the gladiators and other amusements of the time. While in this theatre, he suddenly sees the woman that he wanted to see, the woman whose figure was preserved in the Naples museum. After the theatre, he is invited to her house; and everything is very delightful until suddenly the girl's father appears on the scene. The old man is a Christian, and he is very angry that the ghost of his daughter should deceive a young man in this manner. He makes a sign of the cross, and immediately poor Arria crumbles into dust, and the young man finds himself alone in the ruins of Pompeii. Very beautiful this story is; but every detail in it is dream study.

I have given so much mention to it only because it seems to me the very finest French example of this artistic use of dream experience. But how many other romances belong to the same category? I need only mention among others Irving's "The Adalantado of the Seven Cities," which is pure dream, so realistically told that it gives the reader the sensation of being asleep. Although such romances as "The Seven Sleepers," "Rip Van Winkle," and "Urashima," are not, on the other hand, pure dreams, yet the charm of them is just in that part where dream experience is used. The true romance in all is in the old man's dream of being young, and waking up to cold and grave realities. By the way, in the old French lays of Marie de France, there is an almost precisely similar story to the Japanese one—similar, at least, at all points except the story of the tortoise. It is utterly impossible that the oriental and the occidental story-tellers could have, either of them, borrowed from the other; more probably each story is a spontaneous growth. But it is curious to find the legend substantially the same in other literatures—Indian and Arabian and Javanese. In all of the versions the one romantic truth is ever the same—a dream truth.

Now besides the artistic elements of terror and of romance, dreams certainly furnish us with the most penetrating and beautiful qualities of ghostly tenderness that literature contains. For the dead people that we loved all come back to us occasionally in dreams, and look and talk as if they were actually alive, and become to us everything that we could have wished them to be. In a dream-meeting with the dead, you must have observed how everything is gentle and beautiful, and yet how real, how true it seems. From the most ancient times such visions of the dead have furnished literature with the most touching and the most exquisite passages of unselfish affection. We find this experience in nearly all the ancient ballad-literature of Europe; we find it in all the world's epics; we find it in every kind of superior poetry; and modern literature draws from it more and more as the years go by. Even in such strange compositions as the "Kalevala" of the Finns, an epic totally unlike any other ever written in this world, the one really beautiful passage in an emotional sense is the coming back of the dead mother to comfort the wicked son, which is a dream study, though not so represented in the poem.

Yet one thing more. Our dreams of heaven, what are they in literature but reflections in us of the more beautiful class of dreams? In the world of sleep all the dead people we loved meet us again; the father recovers his long-buried child, the husband his lost wife, separated lovers find the union that was impossible in this world, those whom we lost night of in early years—dead sisters, brothers, friends—all come back to us just as they were then, just as loving, and as young, and perhaps even more beautiful than they could really have been. In the world of sleep there is no growing old; there is immortality, there is everlasting youth. And again how soft, how happy everything is; even the persons unkind to us in waking life become affectionate to us in dreams. Well, what is heaven but this? Religion in painting perfect happiness for the good, only describes the best of our dream life, which is also the best of our waking life; and I think you will find that the closer religion has kept to dream experience in these descriptions, the happier has been the result. Perhaps you will say that I have forgotten how religion teaches the apparition of supernatural powers of a very peculiar kind. But I think that you will find the suggestion for these powers also in dream life. Do we not pass through the air in dreams, pass through solid substances, perform all kinds of miracles, achieve all sorts of impossible things? I think we do. At all events, I am certain that when, as men-of-letters, you have to deal with any form of supernatural subject—whether terrible, or tender, or pathetic, or splendid—you will do well, if you have a good imagination, not to trust to books for your inspiration. Trust to your own dream-life; study it carefully, and draw your inspiration from that. For dreams are the primary source of almost everything that is beautiful in the literature which treats of what lies beyond mere daily experience.

INTRODUCTION

Four tales are, it is said, intended by the Author to be appropriate to the Four Seasons: the stern, grave "Sintram", to winter; the tearful, smiling, fresh "Undine", to Spring; the torrid deserts of the "Two Captains", to summer; and the sunset gold of "Aslauga's Knight", to autumn. Of these two are before us.

The author of these tales, as well as of many more, was Friedrich, Baron de la Motte Fouque, one of the foremost of the minstrels or tale-tellers of the realm of spiritual chivalry—the realm whither Arthur's knights departed when they "took the Sancgreal's holy quest,"—whence Spenser's Red Cross knight and his fellows came forth on their adventures, and in which the Knight of la Mancha believed, and endeavoured to exist.

La Motte Fouque derived his name and his title from the French Huguenot ancestry, who had fled on the Revocation of the Edict of Nantes. His Christian name was taken from his godfather, Frederick the Great, of whom his father was a faithful friend, without compromising his religious principles and practice. Friedrich was born at Brandenburg on February 12, 1777, was educated by good parents at home, served in the Prussian army through disaster and success, took an enthusiastic part in the rising of his country against Napoleon, inditing as many battle-songs as Korner. When victory was achieved, he dedicated his sword in the church of Neunhausen where his estate lay. He lived there, with his beloved wife and his imagination, till his death in 1843.

And all the time life was to him a poet's dream. He lived in a continual glamour of spiritual romance, bathing everything, from the old deities of the Valhalla down to the champions of German liberation, in an ideal glow of purity and nobleness, earnestly Christian throughout, even in his dealings with Northern mythology, for he saw Christ unconsciously shown in Baldur, and Satan in Loki.

Thus he lived, felt, and believed what he wrote, and though his dramas and poems do not rise above fair mediocrity, and the great number of his prose stories are injured by a certain monotony, the charm of them is in their elevation of sentiment and the earnest faith pervading all. His knights might be Sir Galahad—

"My strength is as the strength of ten,
Because my heart is pure."

Evil comes to them as something to be conquered, generally as a form of magic enchantment, and his "wondrous fair maidens" are worthy of them. Yet there is adventure enough to afford much pleasure, and often we have a touch of true genius, which has given actual ideas to the world, and precious ones.

This genius is especially traceable in his two masterpieces, Sintram and Undine. Sintram was inspired by Albert Durer's engraving of the "Knight of Death," of which we give a presentation. It was sent to Fouque by his friend Edward Hitzig, with a request that he would compose a ballad on it. The date of the engraving is 1513, and we quote the description given by the late Rev. R. St. John Tyrwhitt, showing how differently it may be read.

"Some say it is the end of the strong wicked man, just overtaken by Death and Sin, whom he has served on earth. It is said that the tuft on the lance indicates his murderous character, being of such unusual size. You know the use of that appendage was to prevent blood running down from the spearhead to the hands. They also think that the object under the horse's off hind foot is a snare, into which the old oppressor is to fall instantly. The expression of the faces may be taken either way: both good men and bad may have hard, regular features; and both good men and bad would set their teeth grimly on seeing Death, with the sands of their life nearly run out. Some say they think the expression of Death gentle, or only admonitory (as the author of "Sintram"); and I have to thank the authoress of the "Heir of Redclyffe" for showing me a fine impression of the plate, where Death certainly had a not ungentle countenance—snakes and all. I think the shouldered lance, and quiet, firm seat on horseback, with gentle bearing on the curb-bit, indicate grave resolution in the rider, and that a robber knight would have his lance in rest; then there is the leafy crown on the horse's head; and the horse and dog move on so quietly, that I am inclined to hope the best for the Ritter."

Musing on the mysterious engraving, Fouque saw in it the life-long companions of man, Death and Sin, whom he must defy in order to reach salvation; and out of that contemplation rose his wonderful romance, not exactly an allegory, where every circumstance can be fitted with an appropriate meaning, but with the sense of the struggle of life, with external temptation and hereditary inclination pervading all, while Grace and Prayer aid the effort. Folko and Gabrielle are revived from the Magic Ring, that Folko may by example and influence enhance all higher resolutions; while Gabrielle, in all unconscious innocence, awakes the passions, and thus makes the conquest the harder.

It is within the bounds of possibility that the similarities of folk-lore may have brought to Fouque's knowledge the outline of the story which Scott tells us was the germ of "Guy Mannering"; where a boy, whose horoscope had been drawn by an astrologer, as likely to encounter peculiar trials at certain intervals, actually had, in his twenty-first year, a sort of visible encounter with the Tempter, and came off conqueror by his strong faith in the Bible. Sir Walter, between reverence and realism, only took the earlier part of the story, but Fouque gives us the positive struggle, and carries us along with the final victory and subsequent peace. His tale has had a remarkable power over the readers. We cannot but mention two remarkable instances at either end of the scale. Cardinal Newman, in his younger days, was so much overcome by it that he hurried out into the garden to read it alone, and returned with traces of emotion in his face. And when Charles Lowder read it to his East End boys, their whole minds seemed engrossed by it, and they even called certain spots after the places mentioned. Imagine the Rocks of the Moon in Ratcliff Highway!

May we mention that Miss Christabel Coleridge's "Waynflete" brings something of the spirit and idea of "Sintram" into modern life?

"Undine" is a story of much lighter fancy, and full of a peculiar grace, though with a depth of melancholy that endears it. No doubt it was founded on the universal idea in folk-lore of the nixies or water-spirits, one of whom, in Norwegian legend, was seen weeping bitterly because of the want of a soul. Sometimes the nymph is a wicked siren like the Lorelei; but in many of these tales she weds an earthly lover, and deserts him after a time, sometimes on finding her diving cap, or her seal-skin garment, which restores her to her ocean kindred, sometimes on his intruding on her while she is under a periodical transformation, as with the fairy Melusine, more rarely if he becomes unfaithful.

There is a remarkable Cornish tale of a nymph or mermaiden, who thus vanished, leaving a daughter who loved to linger on the beach rather than sport with other children. By and by she had a lover, but no sooner did he show tokens of inconstancy, than the mother came up from the sea and put him to death, when the daughter pined away and died. Her name was Selina, which gives the tale a modern aspect, and makes us wonder if the old tradition can have been modified by some report of Undine's story.

There was an idea set forth by the Rosicrucians of spirits abiding in the elements, and as Undine represented the water influences, Fouque's wife, the Baroness Caroline, wrote a fairly pretty story on the sylphs of fire. But Undine's freakish playfulness and mischief as an elemental being, and her sweet patience when her soul is won, are quite original, and indeed we cannot help sharing, or at least understanding, Huldbrand's beginning to shrink from the unearthly creature to something of his own flesh and blood. He is altogether unworthy, and though in this tale there is far less of spiritual meaning than in Sintram, we cannot but see that Fouque's thought was that the grosser human nature is unable to appreciate what is absolutely pure and unearthly.

C. M. YONGE

UNDINE

CHAPTER I

On a beautiful evening, many hundred years ago, a worthy old fisherman sat mending his nets. The spot where he dwelt was exceedingly picturesque. The green turf on which he had built his cottage ran far out into a great lake; and this slip of verdure appeared to stretch into it as much through love of its clear waters as the lake, moved by a like impulse, strove to fold the meadow, with its waving grass and flowers, and the cooling shade of the trees, in its embrace of love. They seemed to be drawn toward each other, and the one to be visiting the other as a guest.

With respect to human beings, indeed, in this pleasant spot, excepting the fisherman and his family, there were few, or rather none, to be met with. For as in the background of the scene, toward the west and north-west, lay a forest of extraordinary wildness, which, owing to its sunless gloom and almost impassable recesses, as well as to fear of the strange creatures and visionary illusions to be encountered in it, most people avoided entering, unless in cases of extreme necessity. The pious old fisherman, however, many times passed through it without harm, when he carried the fine fish which he caught by his beautiful strip of land to a great city lying only a short distance beyond the forest.

Now the reason he was able to go through this wood with so

much ease may have been chiefly this, because he entertained scarcely any thoughts but such as were of a religious nature; and besides, every time he crossed the evil-reported shades, he used to sing some holy song with a clear voice and from a sincere heart.

Well, while he sat by his nets this evening, neither fearing nor devising evil, a sudden terror seized him, as he heard a rushing in the darkness of the wood, that resembled the tramping of a mounted steed, and the noise continued every instant drawing nearer and nearer to his little territory.

What he had fancied, when abroad in many a stormy night, respecting the mysteries of the forest, now flashed through his mind in a moment, especially the figure of a man of gigantic stature and snow-white appearance, who kept nodding his head in a portentous manner. And when he raised his eyes towards the wood, the form came before him in perfect distinctness, as he saw the nodding man burst forth from the mazy web-work of leaves and branches. But he immediately felt emboldened, when he reflected that nothing to give him alarm had ever befallen him even in the forest; and moreover, that on this open neck of land the evil spirit, it was likely, would be still less daring in the exercise of his power. At the same time he prayed aloud with the most earnest sincerity of devotion, repeating a passage of the Bible. This inspired him with fresh courage, and soon perceiving the illusion, and the strange mistake into which his imagination had betrayed him, he could with difficulty refrain from laughing. The white nodding figure he had seen became transformed, in the twinkling of an eye, to what in reality it was, a small brook, long and familiarly known to him, which ran foaming from the forest, and discharged itself into the lake.

But what had caused the startling sound was a knight arrayed in sumptuous apparel, who from under the shadows of the trees came riding toward the cottage. His doublet was violet embroidered with gold, and his scarlet cloak hung gracefully over it; on his cap of burnished gold waved red and violet-coloured plumes; and in his golden shoulder-belt flashed a sword, richly ornamented, and extremely beautiful. The white barb that bore the knight was more slenderly built than war-horses usually are, and he touched the turf with a step so light and elastic that the green and flowery carpet seemed hardly to receive the slightest injury from his tread. The old fisherman, notwithstanding, did not feel perfectly secure in his mind, although he was forced to believe that no evil could be feared from an appearance so pleasing, and therefore, as good manners dictated, he took off his hat on the knight's coming near, and quietly remained by the side of his nets.

When the stranger stopped, and asked whether he, with his horse, could have shelter and entertainment there for the night, the fisherman returned answer: "As to your horse, fair sir, I have no better stable for him than this shady meadow, and no better provender than the grass that is growing here. But with respect to yourself, you shall be welcome to our humble cottage, and to the best supper and lodging we are able to give you."

The knight was well contented with this reception; and alighting from his horse, which his host assisted him to relieve from saddle and bridle, he let him hasten away to the fresh pasture, and thus spoke: "Even had I found you less hospitable and kindly disposed, my worthy old friend, you would still, I suspect, hardly have got rid of me to-day; for here, I perceive, a broad lake lies before us, and as to riding back into that wood of wonders, with the shades of evening deepening around me, may Heaven in its grace preserve me from the thought."

"Pray, not a word of the wood, or of returning into it!" said the fisherman, and took his guest into the cottage.

There beside the hearth, from which a frugal fire was diffusing its light through the clean twilight room, sat the fisherman's aged wife in a great chair. At the entrance of their noble guest, she rose and gave him a courteous welcome, but sat down again in her seat of honour, not making the slightest offer of it to the stranger. Upon this the fisherman said with a smile:

"You must not be offended with her, young gentleman, because she has not given up to you the best chair in the house; it is a custom among poor people to look upon this as the privilege of the aged."

"Why, husband!" cried the old lady, with a quiet smile, "where can your wits be wandering? Our guest, to say the least of him, must belong to a Christian country; and how is it possible, then, that so well-bred a young man as he appears to be could dream of driving old people from their chairs? Take a seat, my young master," continued she, turning to the knight; "there is still quite a snug little chair on the other side of the room there, only be careful not to shove it about too roughly, for one of its legs, I fear, is none of the firmest."

The knight brought up the seat as carefully as she could desire, sat down upon it good-humouredly, and it seemed to him almost as if he must be somehow related to this little household, and have just returned home from abroad.

These three worthy people now began to converse in the most friendly and familiar manner. In relation to the forest, indeed, concerning which the knight occasionally made some inquiries, the old man chose to know and say but little; he was of opinion that slightly touching upon it at this hour of twilight was most suitable and safe; but of the cares and comforts of their home, and their business abroad, the aged couple spoke more freely, and listened also with eager curiosity as the knight recounted to them his travels, and how he had a castle near one of the sources of the Danube, and that his name was Sir Huldbrand of Ringstetten.

Already had the stranger, while they were in the midst of their talk, heard at times a splash against the little low window, as if some one were dashing water against it. The old man, every time he heard the noise, knit his brows with vexation; but at last, when the whole sweep of a shower came pouring like a torrent against the panes, and bubbling through the decayed frame into the room, he started up indignant, rushed to the window, and cried with a threatening voice—

"Undine! will you never leave off these fooleries?—not even to-day, when we have a stranger knight with us in the cottage?"

All without now became still, only a low laugh was just audible, and the fisherman said, as he came back to his seat, "You will have the goodness, my honoured guest, to pardon this freak, and it may be a multitude more; but she has no thought of evil or of any harm. This mischievous Undine, to confess the truth, is our adopted daughter, and she stoutly refuses to give over this frolicsome childishness of hers, although she has already entered her eighteenth year. But in spite of this, as I said before, she is at heart one of the very best children in the world."

"YOU may say so," broke in the old lady, shaking her head; "you can give a better account of her than I can. When you return home from fishing, or from selling your fish in the city, you may think her frolics very delightful, but to have her dancing about you the whole day long, and never from morning to night to hear her speak one word of sense; and then as she grows older, instead of having any help from her in the family, to find her a continual cause of anxiety, lest her wild humours should completely ruin us, that is quite another thing, and enough at last to weary out the patience even of a saint."

"Well, well," replied the master of the house with a smile, "you have your trials with Undine, and I have mine with the lake. The lake often beats down my dams, and breaks the meshes of my nets, but for all that I have a strong affection for it, and so have you, in spite of your mighty crosses and vexations, for our graceful little child. Is it not true?"

"One cannot be very angry with her," answered the old lady, as she gave her husband an approving smile.

That instant the door flew open, and a fair girl, of wondrous beauty, sprang laughing in, and said, "You have only been making a mock of me, father; for where now is the guest you mentioned?"

The same moment, however, she perceived the knight

also, and continued standing before the young man in fixed astonishment. Huldbrand was charmed with her graceful figure, and viewed her lovely features with the more intense interest, as he imagined it was only her surprise that allowed him the opportunity, and that she would soon turn away from his gaze with increased bashfulness. But the event was the very reverse of what he expected; for, after looking at him for a long while, she became more confident, moved nearer, knelt down before him, and while she played with a gold medal which he wore attached to a rich chain on his breast, exclaimed,

"Why, you beautiful, you kind guest! how have you reached our poor cottage at last? Have you been obliged for years and years to wander about the world before you could catch one glimpse of our nook? Do you come out of that wild forest, my beautiful knight?"

The old woman was so prompt in her reproof as to allow him no time to answer. She commanded the maiden to rise, show better manners, and go to her work. But Undine, without making any reply, drew a little footstool near Huldbrand's chair, sat down upon it with her netting, and said in a gentle tone—

"I will work here."

The old man did as parents are apt to do with children to whom they have been over-indulgent. He affected to observe nothing of Undine's strange behaviour, and was beginning to talk about something else. But this the maiden did not permit him to do. She broke in upon him, "I have asked our kind guest from whence he has come among us, and he has not yet answered me."

"I come out of the forest, you lovely little vision," Huldbrand returned; and she spoke again:

"You must also tell me how you came to enter that forest, so feared and shunned, and the marvellous adventures you met with in it; for there is no escaping without something of this kind."

Huldbrand felt a slight shudder on remembering what he

had witnessed, and looked involuntarily toward the window, for it seemed to him that one of the strange shapes which had come upon him in the forest must be there grinning in through the glass; but he discerned nothing except the deep darkness of night, which had now enveloped the whole prospect. Upon this he became more collected, and was just on the point of beginning his account, when the old man thus interrupted him:

"Not so, sir knight; this is by no means a fit hour for such relations."

But Undine, in a state of high excitement, sprang up from her little stool and cried, placing herself directly before the fisherman: "He shall NOT tell his story, father? he shall not? But it is my will:—he shall!—stop him who may!"

Thus speaking, she stamped her little foot vehemently on the floor, but all with an air of such comic and good-humoured simplicity, that Huldbrand now found it quite as hard to withdraw his gaze from her wild emotion as he had before from her gentleness and beauty. The old man, on the contrary, burst out in unrestrained displeasure. He severely reproved Undine for her disobedience and her unbecoming carriage towards the stranger, and his good old wife joined him in harping on the same string.

By these rebukes Undine was only excited the more. "If you want to quarrel with me," she cried, "and will not let me hear what I so much desire, then sleep alone in your smoky old hut!" And swift as an arrow she shot from the door, and vanished amid the darkness of the night.

Huldbrand and the fisherman sprang from their seats, and were rushing to stop the angry girl; but before they could reach the cottage-door, she had disappeared in the stormy darkness without, and no sound, not so much even as that of her light footstep, betrayed the course she had taken. Huldbrand threw a glance of inquiry towards his host; it almost seemed to him as if the whole of the sweet apparition, which had so suddenly plunged again amid the night, were no other than a continuation of the wonderful forms that had just played their mad pranks with him in the forest. But the old man muttered between his teeth,

"This is not the first time she has treated us in this manner. Now must our hearts be filled with anxiety, and our eyes find no sleep for the whole night; for who can assure us, in spite of her past escapes, that she will not some time or other come to harm, if she thus continue out in the dark and alone until daylight?"

"Then pray, for God's sake, father, let us follow her," cried Huldbrand anxiously.

"Wherefore should we?" replied the old man. "It would be a sin were I to suffer you, all alone, to search after the foolish girl amid the lonesomeness of night; and my old limbs would fail to carry me to this wild rover, even if I knew to what place she has betaken herself."

"Still we ought at least to call after her, and beg her to return," said Huldbrand; and he began to call in tones of earnest entreaty, "Undine! Undine! come back, come back!"

The old man shook his head, and said, "All your shouting, however loud and long, will be of no avail; you know not as yet, sir knight, how self-willed the little thing is." But still, even hoping against hope, he could not himself cease calling out every minute, amid the gloom of night, "Undine! ah, dear Undine! I beseech you, pray come back—only this once."

It turned out, however, exactly as the fisherman had said. No Undine could they hear or see; and as the old man would on no account consent that Huldbrand should go in quest of the fugitive, they were both obliged at last to return into the cottage. There they found the fire on the hearth almost gone out, and the mistress of the house, who took Undine's flight and danger far less to heart than her husband, had already gone to rest. The old man blew up the coals, put on dry wood, and by the firelight hunted for a flask of wine, which he brought and set between himself and his guest.

"You, sir knight, as well as I," said he, "are anxious on the silly girl's account; and it would be better, I think, to spend part of the night in chatting and drinking, than keep turning and turning on our rush-mats, and trying in vain to sleep. What is your opinion?"

Huldbrand was well pleased with the plan; the fisherman pressed him to take the empty seat of honour, its late occupant having now left it for her couch; and they relished their beverage and enjoyed their chat as two such good men and true ever ought to do. To be sure, whenever the slightest thing moved before the windows, or at times when even nothing was moving, one of them would look up and exclaim, "Here she comes!" Then would they continue silent a few moments, and afterward, when nothing appeared, would shake their heads, breathe out a sigh, and go on with their talk.

But, as neither could think of anything but Undine, the best plan they could devise was, that the old fisherman should relate, and the knight should hear, in what manner Undine had come to the cottage. So the fisherman began as follows:

"It is now about fifteen years since I one day crossed the wild forest with fish for the city market. My wife had remained at home as she was wont to do; and at this time for a reason of more than common interest, for although we were beginning to feel the advances of age, God had bestowed upon us an infant of wonderful beauty. It was a little girl; and we already began to ask ourselves the question, whether we ought not, for the advantage of the new-comer, to quit our solitude, and, the better to bring up this precious gift of Heaven, to remove to some more inhabited place. Poor people, to be sure, cannot in these cases do all you may think they ought, sir knight; but we must all do what we can.

"Well, I went on my way, and this affair would keep running in my head. This slip of land was most dear to me, and I trembled when, amidst the bustle and broils of the city, I thought to myself, 'In a scene of tumult like this, or at least in one not much more quiet, I must soon take up my abode.' But I did not for this murmur against our good God; on the contrary, I praised Him in silence for the new-born babe. I should also speak an untruth, were I to say that anything befell me, either on my passage through the forest to the city, or on my returning homeward, that gave me more alarm than usual, as at that time I had never seen any appearance there which could terrify or annoy me. The Lord was ever with me in those awful shades."

Thus speaking he took his cap reverently from his bald head, and continued to sit for a considerable time in devout thought. He then covered himself again, and went on with his relation.

"On this side the forest, alas! it was on this side, that woe burst upon me. My wife came wildly to meet me, clad in mourning apparel, and her eyes streaming with tears. 'Gracious God!' I cried, 'where's our child? Speak!'

"'With Him on whom you have called, dear husband,' she answered, and we now entered the cottage together, weeping in silence. I looked for the little corpse, almost fearing to find what I was seeking; and then it was I first learnt how all had happened.

"My wife had taken the little one in her arms, and walked out to the shore of the lake. She there sat down by its very brink; and while she was playing with the infant, as free from all fear as she was full of delight, it bent forward on a sudden, as if seeing something very beautiful in the water. My wife saw her laugh, the dear angel, and try to catch the image in her tiny hands; but in a moment—with a motion swifter than sight—she sprang from her mother's arms, and sank in the lake, the watery glass into which she had been gazing. I searched for our lost darling again and again; but it was all in vain; I could nowhere find the least trace of her.

"The same evening we childless parents were sitting together by our cottage hearth. We had no desire to talk, even if our tears would have permitted us. As we thus sat in mournful stillness, gazing into the fire, all at once we heard something without,—a slight rustling at the door. The door flew open, and we saw a little girl, three or four years old, and more beautiful than I can say, standing on the threshold, richly dressed, and smiling upon us. We were struck dumb with astonishment, and I knew not for a time whether the tiny form were a real human being, or a mere mockery of enchantment. But I soon perceived water dripping from her golden hair and rich garments, and that the pretty child had been lying in the water, and stood in immediate need of our help.

"'Wife,' said I, 'no one has been able to save our child for us; but let us do for others what would have made us so blessed could any one have done it for us.'

"We undressed the little thing, put her to bed, and gave her something to drink; at all this she spoke not a word, but only turned her eyes upon us—eyes blue and bright as sea or sky— and continued looking at us with a smile.

"Next morning we had no reason to fear that she had received any other harm than her wetting, and I now asked her about her parents, and how she could have come to us. But the account she gave was both confused and incredible. She must surely have been born far from here, not only because I have been unable for these fifteen years to learn anything of her birth, but because she then said, and at times continues to say, many things of so very singular a nature, that we neither of us know, after all, whether she may not have dropped among us from the moon; for her talk runs upon golden castles, crystal domes, and Heaven knows what extravagances beside. What, however, she related with most distinctness was this: that while she was once taking a sail with her mother on the great lake, she fell out of the boat into the water; and that when she first recovered her senses, she was here under our trees, where the gay scenes of the shore filled her with delight.

"We now had another care weighing upon our minds, and one that caused us no small perplexity and uneasiness. We of course very soon determined to keep and bring up the child we had found, in place of our own darling that had been drowned; but who could tell us whether she had been baptized or not? She herself could give us no light on the subject. When we asked her the question, she commonly made answer, that she well knew she was created for God's praise and glory, and that she was willing to let us do with her all that might promote His glory and praise.

"My wife and I reasoned in this way: 'If she has not been baptized, there can be no use in putting off the ceremony; and if she has been, it still is better to have too much of a good thing than too little.'

"Taking this view of our difficulty, we now endeavoured to hit upon a good name for the child, since, while she remained without one, we were often at a loss, in our familiar talk, to know what to call her. We at length agreed that Dorothea would be most suitable for her, as I had somewhere heard it said that this name signified a gift of God, and surely she had been sent to us by Providence as a gift, to comfort us in our misery. She, on the contrary, would not so much as hear Dorothea mentioned; she insisted, that as she had been named Undine by her parents, Undine she ought still to be called. It now occurred to me that this was a heathenish name, to be found in no calendar, and I resolved to ask the advice of a priest in the city. He would not listen to the name of Undine; and yielding to my urgent request, he came with me through the enchanted forest in order to perform the rite of baptism here in my cottage.

"The little maid stood before us so prettily adorned, and with such an air of gracefulness, that the heart of the priest softened at once in her presence; and she coaxed him so sweetly, and jested with him so merrily, that he at last remembered nothing of his many objections to the name of Undine.

"Thus, then, was she baptized Undine; and during the holy ceremony she behaved with great propriety and gentleness, wild and wayward as at other times she invariably was; for in this my wife was quite right, when she mentioned the anxiety the child has occasioned us. If I should relate to you—"

At this moment the knight interrupted the fisherman, to

direct his attention to a deep sound as of a rushing flood, which had caught his ear during the talk of the old man. And now the waters came pouring on with redoubled fury before the cottage-windows. Both sprang to the door. There they saw, by the light of the now risen moon, the brook which issued from the wood rushing wildly over its banks, and whirling onward with it both stones and branches of trees in its rapid course. The storm, as if awakened by the uproar, burst forth from the clouds, whose immense masses of vapour coursed over the moon with the swiftness of thought; the lake roared beneath the wind that swept the foam from its waves; while the trees of this narrow peninsula groaned from root to topmost branch as they bowed and swung above the torrent.

"Undine! in God's name, Undine!" cried the two men in an agony. No answer was returned. And now, regardless of everything else, they hurried from the cottage, one in this direction, the other in that, searching and calling.

CHAPTER II

The longer Huldbrand sought Undine beneath the shades of night, and failed to find her, the more anxious and confused he became. The impression that she was a mere phantom of the forest gained a new ascendency over him; indeed, amid the howling of the waves and the tempest, the crashing of the trees, and the entire change of the once so peaceful and beautiful scene, he was tempted to view the whole peninsula, together with the cottage and its inhabitants, as little more than some mockery of his senses. But still he heard afar off the fisherman's anxious and incessant shouting, "Undine!" and also his aged wife, who was praying and singing psalms.

At length, when he drew near to the brook, which had overflowed its banks, he perceived by the moonlight, that it had taken its wild course directly in front of the haunted forest, so as to change the peninsula into an island.

"Merciful God!" he breathed to himself, "if Undine has ventured a step within that fearful wood, what will become of her? Perhaps it was all owing to her sportive and wayward spirit, because I would give her no account of my adventures there. And now the stream is rolling between us, she may be weeping alone on the other side in the midst of spectral horrors!"

A shuddering groan escaped him; and clambering over some stones and trunks of overthrown pines, in order to step into the impetuous current, he resolved, either by wading or swimming, to seek the wanderer on the further shore. He felt, it is true, all the dread and shrinking awe creeping over him which he had already suffered by daylight among the now tossing and roaring branches of the forest. More than all, a tall man in white, whom he knew but too well, met his view, as he stood grinning and nodding on the grass beyond the water. But even monstrous forms like this only impelled him to cross over toward them, when the thought rushed upon him that Undine might be there alone and in the agony of death.

He had already grasped a strong branch of a pine, and stood supporting himself upon it in the whirling current, against which he could with difficulty keep himself erect; but he advanced deeper in with a courageous spirit. That instant a gentle voice of warning cried near him, "Do not venture, do not venture!—that OLD MAN, the STREAM, is too full of tricks to be trusted!" He knew the soft tones of the voice; and while he stood as it were entranced beneath the shadows which had now duskily veiled the moon, his head swam with the swelling and rolling of the waves as he saw them momentarily rising above his knee. Still he disdained the thought of giving up his purpose.

"If you are not really there, if you are merely gambolling round me like a mist, may I, too, bid farewell to life, and become a shadow like you, dear, dear Undine!" Thus calling aloud, he again moved deeper into the stream. "Look round you—ah, pray look round you, beautiful young stranger! why rush on death so madly?" cried the voice a second time close by him; and looking on one side he perceived, by the light of the moon, again cloudless, a little island formed by the flood; and crouching upon its flowery turf, beneath the branches of embowering trees, he saw the smiling and lovely Undine.

O how much more gladly than before the young man now plied his sturdy staff! A few steps, and he had crossed the flood that was rushing between himself and the maiden; and he stood near her on the little spot of greensward in security, protected by the old trees. Undine half rose, and she threw her arms around his neck to draw him gently down upon the soft seat by her side.

"Here you shall tell me your story, my beautiful friend," she breathed in a low whisper; "here the cross old people cannot disturb us; and, besides, our roof of leaves here will make quite as good a shelter as their poor cottage."

"It is heaven itself," cried Huldbrand; and folding her in his arms, he kissed the lovely girl with fervour.

The old fisherman, meantime, had come to the margin of the stream, and he shouted across, "Why, how is this, sir knight! I received you with the welcome which one true-hearted man gives to another; and now you sit there caressing my foster-child in secret, while you suffer me in my anxiety to wander through the night in quest of her."

"Not till this moment did I find her myself, old father," cried the knight across the water.

"So much the better," said the fisherman, "but now make haste, and bring her over to me upon firm ground."

To this, however, Undine would by no means consent. She declared that she would rather enter the wild forest itself with the beautiful stranger, than return to the cottage where she was so thwarted in her wishes, and from which the knight would soon or late go away. Then, throwing her arms round Huldbrand, she sang the following verse with the warbling sweetness of a bird:

"A rill would leave its misty vale,
And fortunes wild explore,
Weary at length it reached the main,
And sought its vale no more."

The old fisherman wept bitterly at her song, but his emotion seemed to awaken little or no sympathy in her. She kissed and caressed her new friend, who at last said to her: "Undine, if the distress of the old man does not touch your heart, it cannot but move mine. We ought to return to him."

She opened her large blue eyes upon him in amazement, and spoke at last with a slow and doubtful accent, "If you think so, it is well, all is right to me which you think right. But the old man over there must first give me his promise that he will allow you, without objection, to relate what you saw in the wood, and— well, other things will settle themselves."

"Come—only come!" cried the fisherman to her, unable to utter another word. At the same time he stretched his arms wide over the current towards her, and to give her assurance that he would do what she required, nodded his head. This motion caused his white hair to fall strangely over his face, and Huldbrand could not but remember the nodding white man of the forest. Without allowing anything, however, to produce in him the least confusion, the young knight took the beautiful girl in his arms, and bore her across the narrow channel which the stream had torn away between her little island and the solid shore. The old man fell upon Undine's neck, and found it impossible either to express his joy or to kiss her enough; even the ancient dame came up and embraced the recovered girl most cordially. Every word of censure was carefully avoided; the more so, indeed, as even Undine, forgetting her waywardness, almost overwhelmed her foster-parents with caresses and the prattle of tenderness.

When at length the excess of their joy at recovering their child had subsided, morning had already dawned, shining upon the waters of the lake; the tempest had become hushed, the small birds sung merrily on the moist branches.

As Undine now insisted upon hearing the recital of the knight's promised adventures, the aged couple readily agreed to her wish. Breakfast was brought out beneath the trees which stood behind the cottage toward the lake on the north, and they sat down to it with contented hearts; Undine at the knight's feet on the grass. These arrangements being made, Huldbrand began his story in the following manner:—

"It is now about eight days since I rode into the free imperial city which lies yonder on the farther side of the forest. Soon after my arrival a splendid tournament and running at the ring took place there, and I spared neither my horse nor my lance in the encounters.

"Once while I was pausing at the lists to rest from the brisk exercise, and was handing back my helmet to one of my attendants, a female figure of extraordinary beauty caught my attention, as, most magnificently attired, she stood looking on at one of the balconies. I learned, on making inquiry of a person near me, that the name of the young lady was Bertalda, and that she was a foster-daughter of one of the powerful dukes of this country. She too, I observed, was gazing at me, and the consequences were such as we young knights are wont to experience; whatever success in riding I might have had before, I was now favoured with still better fortune. That evening I was Bertalda's partner in the dance, and I enjoyed the same distinction during the remainder of the festival."

A sharp pain in his left hand, as it hung carelessly beside him, here interrupted Huldbrand's relation, and drew his eye to the part affected. Undine had fastened her pearly teeth, and not without some keenness too, upon one of his fingers, appearing at the same time very gloomy and displeased. On a sudden, however, she looked up in his eyes with an expression of tender melancholy, and whispered almost inaudibly,—

"It is all your own fault."

She then covered her face; and the knight, strangely embarrassed and thoughtful, went on with his story.

"This lady, Bertalda, of whom I spoke, is of a proud and wayward spirit. The second day I saw her she pleased me by no means so much as she had the first, and the third day still less. But I continued about her because she showed me more favour than she did any other knight, and it so happened that I playfully asked her to give me one of her gloves. 'When you have entered the haunted forest all alone,' said she; 'when you have explored its wonders, and brought me a full account of them, the glove is yours.' As to getting her glove, it was of no importance to me whatever, but the word had been spoken, and no honourable knight would permit himself to be urged to such a proof of valour a second time."

"I thought," said Undine, interrupting him, "that she loved you."

"It did appear so," replied Huldbrand.

"Well!" exclaimed the maiden, laughing, "this is beyond

belief; she must be very stupid. To drive from her one who was dear to her! And worse than all, into that ill-omened wood! The wood and its mysteries, for all I should have cared, might have waited long enough."

"Yesterday morning, then," pursued the knight, smiling kindly upon Undine, "I set out from the city, my enterprise before me. The early light lay rich upon the verdant turf. It shone so rosy on the slender boles of the trees, and there was so merry a whispering among the leaves, that in my heart I could not but laugh at people who feared meeting anything to terrify them in a spot so delicious. 'I shall soon pass through the forest, and as speedily return,' I said to myself, in the overflow of joyous feeling, and ere I was well aware, I had entered deep among the green shades, while of the plain that lay behind me I was no longer able to catch a glimpse.

"Then the conviction for the first time impressed me, that in a forest of so great extent I might very easily become bewildered, and that this, perhaps, might be the only danger which was likely to threaten those who explored its recesses. So I made a halt, and turned myself in the direction of the sun, which had meantime risen somewhat higher, and while I was looking up to observe it, I saw something black among the boughs of a lofty oak. My first thought was, 'It is a bear!' and I grasped my weapon. The object then accosted me from above in a human voice, but in a tone most harsh and hideous: 'If I, overhead here, do not gnaw off these dry branches, Sir Noodle, what shall we have to roast you with when midnight comes?' And with that it grinned, and made such a rattling with the branches that my courser became mad with affright, and rushed furiously forward with me before I had time to see distinctly what sort of a devil's beast it was."

"You must not speak so," said the old fisherman, crossing himself. His wife did the same, without saying a word, and Undine, while her eye sparkled with delight, looked at the knight and said, "The best of the story is, however, that as yet they have not roasted you! Go on, now, you beautiful knight."

The knight then went on with his adventures. "My horse was so wild, that he well-nigh rushed with me against limbs and trunks of trees. He was dripping with sweat through terror, heat, and the violent straining of his muscles. Still he refused to slacken his career. At last, altogether beyond my control, he took his course directly up a stony steep, when suddenly a tall white man flashed before me, and threw himself athwart the way my mad steed was taking. At this apparition he shuddered with new affright, and stopped trembling. I took this chance of recovering my command of him, and now for the first time perceived that my deliverer, so far from being a white man, was only a brook of silver brightness, foaming near me in its descent from the hill, while it crossed and arrested my horse's course with its rush of waters."

"Thanks, thanks, dear brook!" cried Undine, clapping her little hands. But the old man shook his head, and looked down in deep thought.

"Hardly had I well settled myself in my saddle, and got the reins in my grasp again," Huldbrand pursued, "when a wizard-like dwarf of a man was already standing at my side, diminutive and ugly beyond conception, his complexion of a brownish-yellow, and his nose scarcely smaller than the rest of him together. The fellow's mouth was slit almost from ear to ear, and he showed his teeth with a grinning smile of idiot courtesy, while he overwhelmed me with bows and scrapes innumerable. The farce now becoming excessively irksome, I thanked him in the fewest words I could well use, turned about my still trembling charger, and purposed either to seek another adventure, or, should I meet with none, to take my way back to the city; for the sun, during my wild chase, had passed the meridian, and was now hastening toward the west. But this villain of a dwarf sprang at the same instant, and, with a turn as rapid as lightning, stood before my horse again. 'Clear the way there!' I cried fiercely; 'the beast is wild, and will make nothing of running over you.'

"'Ay, ay,' cried the imp with a snarl, and snorting out a laugh still more frightfully idiotic; 'pay me, first pay what you owe me. I stopped your fine little nag for you; without my help, both you and he would be now sprawling below there in that stony ravine. Hu! from what a horrible plunge I've saved you!'

"'Well, don't make any more faces,' said I, 'but take your money and be off, though every word you say is false. It was the brook there, you miserable thing, and not you, that saved me,' and at the same time I dropped a piece of gold into his wizard cap, which he had taken from his head while he was begging before me.

"I then trotted off and left him, but he screamed after me; and on a sudden, with inconceivable quickness, he was close by my side. I started my horse into a gallop. He galloped on with me, though it seemed with great difficulty, and with a strange movement, half ludicrous and half horrible, forcing at the same time every limb and feature into distortion, he held up the gold piece and screamed at every leap, 'Counterfeit! false! false coin! counterfeit!' and such was the strange sound that issued from his hollow breast, you would have supposed that at every scream he must have tumbled upon the ground dead. All this while his disgusting red tongue hung lolling from his mouth.

"I stopped bewildered, and asked, 'What do you mean by this screaming? Take another piece of gold, take two, but leave me.'

"He then began again his hideous salutations of courtesy, and snarled out as before, 'Not gold, it shall not be gold, my young gentleman. I have too much of that trash already, as I will show you in no time.'

"At that moment, and thought itself could not have been more instantaneous, I seemed to have acquired new powers of sight. I could see through the solid green plain, as if it were green glass, and the smooth surface of the earth were round as a globe, and within it I saw crowds of goblins, who were pursuing their pastime and making themselves merry with silver and gold. They were tumbling and rolling about, heads up and heads down; they pelted one another in sport with the precious metals, and with irritating malice blew gold-dust in one another's eyes. My odious companion ordered the others to reach him up a vast quantity of gold; this he showed to me with a laugh, and then flung it again ringing and chinking down the measureless abyss.

"After this contemptuous disregard of gold, he held up the piece I had given him, showing it to his brother goblins below, and they laughed immoderately at a coin so worthless, and hissed me. At last, raising their fingers all smutched with ore, they pointed them at me in scorn; and wilder and wilder, and thicker and thicker, and madder and madder, the crowd were clambering up to where I sat gazing at these wonders. Then terror seized me, as it had before seized my horse. I drove my spurs into his sides, and how far he rushed with me through the forest, during this second of my wild heats, it is impossible to say.

"At last, when I had now come to a dead halt again, the cool of evening was around me. I caught the gleam of a white footpath through the branches of the trees; and presuming it would lead me out of the forest toward the city, I was desirous of working my way into it. But a face, perfectly white and indistinct, with features ever changing, kept thrusting itself out and peering at me between the leaves. I tried to avoid it, but wherever I went, there too appeared the unearthly face. I was maddened with rage at this interruption, and determined to drive my steed at the appearance full tilt, when such a cloud of white foam came rushing upon me and my horse, that we were almost blinded and glad to turn about and escape. Thus from step to step it forced us on, and ever aside from the footpath, leaving us for the most part only one direction open. When we advanced in this, it kept following close behind us, yet did not occasion the smallest harm or inconvenience.

"When at times I looked about me at the form, I perceived that the white face, which had splashed upon us its shower of foam, was resting on a body equally white, and of more than gigantic size. Many a time, too, I received the impression that the whole appearance was nothing more than a wandering stream or torrent; but respecting this I could never attain to any certainty. We both of us, horse and rider, became weary as we shaped our course according to the movements of the white man, who continued nodding his head at us, as if he would say, 'Quite right!' And thus, at length, we came out here, at the edge of the wood, where I saw the fresh turf, the waters of the lake, and your little cottage, and where the tall white man disappeared."

"Well, Heaven be praised that he is gone!" cried the old fisherman; and he now began to talk of how his guest could most conveniently return to his friends in the city. Upon this, Undine began laughing to herself, but so very low that the sound was hardly perceivable. Huldbrand observing it, said, "I thought you were glad to see me here; why, then, do you now appear so happy when our talk turns upon my going away?"

"Because you cannot go away," answered Undine. "Pray make a single attempt; try with a boat, with your horse, or alone, as you please, to cross that forest stream which has burst its bounds; or rather, make no trial at all, for you would be dashed to pieces by the stones and trunks of trees which you see driven on with such violence. And as to the lake, I know that well; even my father dares not venture out with his boat far enough to help you."

Huldbrand rose, smiling, in order to look about and observe whether the state of things were such as Undine had represented it to be. The old man accompanied him, and the maiden went merrily dancing beside them. They found all, in fact, just as Undine had said, and that the knight, whether willing or not willing, must submit to remaining on the island, so lately a peninsula, until the flood should subside.

When the three were now returning to the cottage after their ramble, the knight whispered in the ear of the little maiden, "Well, dear Undine, are you angry at my remaining?"

"Ah," she pettishly replied, "do not speak to me! If I had not bitten you, who knows what fine things you would have put into your story about Bertalda?"

CHAPTER III

It may have happened to thee, my dear reader, after being much driven to and fro in the world, to reach at length a spot where all was well with thee. The love of home and of its peaceful joys, innate to all, again sprang up in thy heart; thou thoughtest that thy home was decked with all the flowers of childhood, and of that purest, deepest love which had grown upon the graves of thy beloved, and that here it was good to live and to build houses. Even if thou didst err, and hast had bitterly to mourn thy error, it is nothing to my purpose, and thou thyself wilt not like to dwell on the sad recollection. But recall those unspeakably sweet feelings, that angelic greeting of peace, and thou wilt be able to understand what was the happiness of the knight Huldbrand during his abode on that narrow slip of land.

He frequently observed, with heartfelt satisfaction, that the forest stream continued every day to swell and roll on with a more impetuous sweep; and this forced him to prolong his stay on the island. Part of the day he wandered about with an old cross-bow, which he found in a corner of the cottage, and had repaired in order to shoot the waterfowl that flew over; and all that he was lucky enough to hit he brought home for a good roast in the kitchen. When he came in with his booty, Undine seldom failed to greet him with a scolding, because he had cruelly deprived the happy joyous little creatures of life as they were sporting above in the blue ocean of the air; nay more, she often wept bitterly when she viewed the water-fowl dead in his hand. But at other times, when he returned without having shot any, she gave him a scolding equally serious, since, owing to his carelessness and want of skill, they must now put up with a dinner of fish. Her playful taunts ever touched his heart with delight; the more so, as she generally strove to make up for her pretended ill-humour with endearing caresses.

The old people saw with pleasure this familiarity of Undine and Huldbrand; they looked upon them as betrothed, or even as married, and living with them in their old age on their island, now torn off from the mainland. The loneliness of his situation strongly impressed also the young Huldbrand with the feeling that he was already Undine's bridegroom. It seemed to him as if, beyond those encompassing floods, there were no other world in existence, or at any rate as if he could never cross them, and again associate with the world of other men; and when at times his grazing steed raised his head and neighed to him, seemingly inquiring after his knightly achievements and reminding him of them, or when his coat-of-arms sternly shone upon him from the embroidery of his saddle and the caparisons of his horse, or when his sword happened to fall from the nail on which it was hanging in the cottage, and flashed on his eye as it slipped from the scabbard in its fall, he quieted the doubts of his mind by saying to himself, "Undine cannot be a fisherman's daughter. She is, in all probability, a native of some remote region, and a member of some illustrious family."

There was one thing, indeed, to which he had a strong aversion: this was to hear the old dame reproving Undine. The wild girl, it is true, commonly laughed at the reproof, making no attempt to conceal the extravagance of her mirth; but it appeared to him like touching his own honour; and still he found it impossible to blame the aged wife of the fisherman, since Undine always deserved at least ten times as many reproofs as she received; so he continued to feel in his heart an affectionate tenderness for the ancient mistress of the house, and his whole life flowed on in the calm stream of contentment.

There came, however, an interruption at last. The fisherman and the knight had been accustomed at dinner, and also in the evening when the wind roared without, as it rarely failed to do towards night, to enjoy together a flask of wine. But now their whole stock, which the fisherman had from time to time brought with him from the city, was at last exhausted, and they were both quite out of humour at the circumstance. That day Undine laughed at them excessively, but they were not disposed to join in her jests with the same gaiety as usual. Toward evening she went out of the cottage, to escape, as she said, the sight of two such long and tiresome faces.

While it was yet twilight, some appearances of a tempest seemed to be again mustering in the sky, and the waves already heaved and roared around them: the knight and the fisherman sprang to the door in terror, to bring home the maiden, remembering the anguish of that night when Huldbrand had first entered the cottage. But Undine met them at the same moment, clapping her little hands in high glee.

"What will you give me," she cried, "to provide you with wine? or rather, you need not give me anything," she continued; "for I am already satisfied, if you look more cheerful, and are in better spirits, than throughout this last most wearisome day. Only come with me; the forest stream has driven ashore a cask; and I will be condemned to sleep through a whole week, if it is not a wine-cask."

The men followed her, and actually found, in a bushy cove of the shore, a cask, which inspired them with as much joy as if they were sure it contained the generous old wine for which they were thirsting. They first of all, and with as much expedition as possible, rolled it toward the cottage; for heavy clouds were again rising in the west, and they could discern the waves of the lake in the fading light lifting their white foaming heads, as if looking out for the rain, which threatened every instant to pour upon them. Undine helped the men as much as she was able; and as the shower, with a roar of wind, came suddenly sweeping on in rapid pursuit, she raised her finger with a merry menace toward the dark mass of clouds, and cried:

"You cloud, you cloud, have a care! beware how you wet us; we are some way from shelter yet."

The old man reproved her for this sally, as a sinful presumption; but she laughed to herself softly, and no mischief came from her wild behaviour. Nay more, what was beyond their expectation, they reached their comfortable hearth unwet, with their prize secured; but the cask had hardly been broached, and proved to contain wine of a remarkably fine flavour, when the rain first poured down unrestrained from the black cloud, the tempest raved through the tops of the trees, and swept far over the billows of the deep.

Having immediately filled several bottles from the cask, which promised them a supply for a long time, they drew round the glowing hearth; and, comfortably secured from the tempest, they sat tasting the flavour of their wine and bandying jests.

But the old fisherman suddenly became extremely grave, and said: "Ah, great God! here we sit, rejoicing over this rich gift, while he to whom it first belonged, and from whom it was wrested by the fury of the stream, must there also, it is more than probable, have lost his life."

"No such thing," said Undine, smiling, as she filled the knight's cup to the brim.

But he exclaimed: "By my unsullied honour, old father, if I knew where to find and rescue him, no fear of exposure to the night, nor any peril, should deter me from making the attempt. At least, I can promise you that if I again reach an inhabited country, I will find out the owner of this wine or his heirs, and make double and triple reimbursement."

The old man was gratified with this assurance; he gave the knight a nod of approbation, and now drained his cup with an easier conscience and more relish.

Undine, however, said to Huldbrand: "As to the repayment and your gold, you may do whatever you like. But what you said about your venturing out, and searching, and exposing yourself to danger, appears to me far from wise. I should cry my very eyes out, should you perish in such a wild attempt; and is it not true that you would prefer staying here with me and the good wine?"

"Most assuredly," answered Huldbrand, smiling.

"Then, you see," replied Undine, "you spoke unwisely. For charity begins at home; and why need we trouble ourselves about our neighbours?"

The mistress of the house turned away from her, sighing and shaking her head; while the fisherman forgot his wonted indulgence toward the graceful maiden, and thus rebuked her:

"That sounds exactly as if you had been brought up by heathens and Turks;" and he finished his reproof by adding, "May God forgive both me and you—unfeeling child!"

"Well, say what you will, that is what I think and feel," replied Undine, "whoever brought me up; and all your talking cannot help it."

"Silence!" exclaimed the fisherman, in a voice of stern rebuke; and she, who with all her wild spirit was extremely alive to fear, shrank from him, moved close up to Huldbrand, trembling, and said very softly:

"Are you also angry, dear friend?"

The knight pressed her soft hand, and tenderly stroked her locks. He was unable to utter a word, for his vexation, arising from the old man's severity towards Undine, closed his lips; and thus the two couples sat opposite to each other, at once heated with anger and in embarrassed silence.

In the midst of this stillness a low knocking at the door startled them all; for there are times when a slight circumstance, coming unexpectedly upon us, startles us like something supernatural. But there was the further source of alarm, that the enchanted forest lay so near them, and that their place of abode seemed at present inaccessible to any human being. While they were looking upon one another in doubt, the knocking was again heard, accompanied with a deep groan. The knight sprang to seize his sword. But the old man said, in a low whisper:

"If it be what I fear it is, no weapon of yours can protect us."

Undine in the meanwhile went to the door, and cried with the firm voice of fearless displeasure: "Spirits of the earth! if mischief be your aim, Kuhleborn shall teach you better manners."

The terror of the rest was increased by this wild speech; they looked fearfully upon the girl, and Huldbrand was just recovering presence of mind enough to ask what she meant, when a voice reached them from without:

"I am no spirit of the earth, though a spirit still in its earthly body. You that are within the cottage there, if you fear God and would afford me assistance, open your door to me."

By the time these words were spoken, Undine had already opened it; and the lamp throwing a strong light upon the stormy night, they perceived an aged priest without, who stepped back in terror, when his eye fell on the unexpected sight of a little damsel of such exquisite beauty. Well might he think there must be magic in the wind and witchcraft at work, when a form of such surpassing loveliness appeared at the door of so humble a dwelling. So he lifted up his voice in prayer:

"Let all good spirits praise the Lord God!"

"I am no spectre," said Undine, with a smile. "Do I look so very frightful? And you see that I do not shrink from holy words. I too have knowledge of God, and understand the duty of praising Him; every one, to be sure, has his own way of doing this, for so He has created us. Come in, father; you will find none but worthy people here."

The holy man came bowing in, and cast round a glance of scrutiny, wearing at the same time a very placid and venerable air. But water was dropping from every fold of his dark garments, from his long white beard and the white locks of his hair. The fisherman and the knight took him to another apartment, and furnished him with a change of raiment, while they gave his own clothes to the women to dry. The aged stranger thanked them in a manner the most humble and courteous; but on the knight's offering him his splendid cloak to wrap round him, he could not be persuaded to take it, but chose instead an old grey coat that belonged to the fisherman.

They then returned to the common apartment. The mistress

of the house immediately offered her great chair to the priest, and continued urging it upon him till she saw him fairly in possession of it. "You are old and exhausted," said she, "and are, moreover, a man of God."

Undine shoved under the stranger's feet her little stool, on which at all other times she used to sit near to Huldbrand, and showed herself most gentle and amiable towards the old man. Huldbrand whispered some raillery in her ear, but she replied, gravely:

"He is a minister of that Being who created us all; and holy things are not to be treated with lightness."

The knight and the fisherman now refreshed the priest with food and wine; and when he had somewhat recovered his strength and spirits, he began to relate how he had the day before set out from his cloister, which was situated far off beyond the great lake, in order to visit the bishop, and acquaint him with the distress into which the cloister and its tributary villages had fallen, owing to the extraordinary floods. After a long and wearisome wandering, on account of the rise of the waters, he had been this day compelled toward evening to procure the aid of a couple of boatmen, and cross over an arm of the lake which had burst its usual boundary.

"But hardly," continued he, "had our small ferry-boat touched the waves, when that furious tempest burst forth which is still raging over our heads. It seemed as if the billows had been waiting our approach only to rush on us with a madness the more wild. The oars were wrested from the grasp of my men in an instant; and shivered by the resistless force, they drove farther and farther out before us upon the waves. Unable to direct our course, we yielded to the blind power of nature, and seemed to fly over the surges toward your distant shore, which we already saw looming through the mist and foam of the deep. Then it was at last that our boat turned short from its course, and rocked with a motion that became more wild and dizzy: I know not whether it was overset, or the violence of the motion threw me overboard. In my agony and struggle at the thought of a near and terrible death, the waves bore me onward, till I was cast ashore here beneath the trees of your island."

"Yes, an island!" cried the fisherman; "a short time ago it was only a point of land. But now, since the forest stream and lake have become all but mad, it appears to be entirely changed."

"I observed something of it," replied the priest, "as I stole along the shore in the obscurity; and hearing nothing around me but a sort of wild uproar, I perceived at last that the noise came from a point exactly where a beaten footpath disappeared. I now caught the light in your cottage, and ventured hither, where I cannot sufficiently thank my Heavenly Father that, after preserving me from the waters, He has also conducted me to such pious people as you are; and the more so, as it is difficult to say whether I shall ever behold any other persons in this world except you four."

"What mean you by those words?" asked the fisherman.

"Can you tell me, then, how long this commotion of the elements will last?" replied the priest. "I am old; the stream of my life may easily sink into the ground and vanish before the overflowing of that forest stream shall subside. And, indeed, it is not impossible that more and more of the foaming waters may rush in between you and yonder forest, until you are so far removed from the rest of the world, that your small fishing-canoe may be incapable of passing over, and the inhabitants of the continent entirely forget you in your old age amid the dissipation and diversions of life."

At this melancholy foreboding the old lady shrank back with a feeling of alarm, crossed herself, and cried, "God forbid!"

But the fisherman looked upon her with a smile and said, "What a strange being is man! Suppose the worst to happen; our state would not be different; at any rate, your own would not, dear wife, from what it is at present. For have you, these many years, been farther from home than the border of the forest? And have you seen a single human being beside Undine and myself? It is now only a short time since the coming of the knight and the priest. They will remain with us, even if we do become a forgotten island; so after all you will be a gainer."

"I know not," replied the ancient dame; "it is a dismal thought, when brought fairly home to the mind, that we are for ever separated from mankind, even though in fact we never do know nor see them."

"Then YOU will remain with us—then you will remain with us!" whispered Undine, in a voice scarcely audible and half singing, while she nestled closer to Huldbrand's side. But he was immersed in the deep and strange musings of his own mind. The region, on the farther side of the forest river, seemed, since the last words of the priest, to have been withdrawing farther and farther, in dim perspective, from his view; and the blooming island on which he lived grew green and smiled more freshly in his fancy. His bride glowed like the fairest rose, not of this obscure nook only, but even of the whole wide world; and the priest was now present.

Added to which, the mistress of the family was directing an angry glance at Undine, because, even in the presence of the priest, she leant so fondly on the knight; and it seemed as if she was on the point of breaking out in harsh reproof. Then burst forth from the mouth of Huldbrand, as he turned to the priest, "Father, you here see before you an affianced pair; and if this maiden and these good old people have no objection, you shall unite us this very evening."

The aged couple were both exceedingly surprised. They had often, it is true, thought of this, but as yet they had never mentioned it; and now, when the knight spoke, it came upon them like something wholly new and unexpected. Undine became suddenly grave, and looked down thoughtfully, while the priest made inquiries respecting the circumstances of their acquaintance, and asked the old people whether they gave their consent to the union. After a great number of questions and answers, the affair was arranged to the satisfaction of all; and the mistress of the house went to prepare the bridal apartment of the young couple, and also, with a view to grace the nuptial solemnity, to seek for two consecrated tapers, which she had for a long time kept by her, for this occasion.

The knight in the meanwhile busied himself about his golden chain, for the purpose of disengaging two of its links, that he might make an exchange of rings with his bride. But when she saw his object, she started from her trance of musing, and exclaimed—

"Not so! my parents by no means sent me into the world so perfectly destitute; on the contrary, they foresaw, even at that early period, that such a night as this would come."

Thus speaking she went out of the room, and a moment after returned with two costly rings, of which she gave one to her bridegroom, and kept the other for herself. The old fisherman was beyond measure astonished at this; and his wife, who was just re-entering the room, was even more surprised than he, that neither of them had ever seen these jewels in the child's possession.

"My parents," said Undine, "sewed these trinkets to that beautiful raiment which I wore the very day I came to you. They also charged me on no account whatever to mention them to any one before my wedding evening. At the time of my coming, therefore, I took them off in secret, and have kept them concealed to the present hour."

The priest now cut short all further questioning and wondering, while he lighted the consecrated tapers, placed them on a table, and ordered the bridal pair to stand opposite to him. He then pronounced the few solemn words of the ceremony, and made them one. The elder couple gave the younger their blessing; and the bride, gently trembling and thoughtful, leaned upon the knight.

The priest then spoke out: "You are strange people, after all; for why did you tell me that you were the only inhabitants of the island? So far is this from being true, I have seen, the whole time

I was performing the ceremony, a tall, stately man, in a white mantle, standing opposite to me, looking in at the window. He must be still waiting before the door, if peradventure you would invite him to come in."

"God forbid!" cried the old lady, shrinking back; the fisherman shook his head, without opening his lips; and Huldbrand sprang to the window. It seemed to him that he could still discern a white streak, which soon disappeared in the gloom. He convinced the priest that he must have been mistaken in his impression; and they all sat down together round a bright and comfortable hearth.

CHAPTER IV

Before the nuptial ceremony, and during its performance, Undine had shown a modest gentleness and maidenly reserve; but it now seemed as if all the wayward freaks that effervesced within her burst forth with an extravagance only the more bold and unrestrained. She teased her bridegroom, her foster-parents, and even the priest, whom she had just now revered so highly, with all sorts of childish tricks; but when the ancient dame was about to reprove her too frolicsome spirit, the knight, in a few words, imposed silence upon her by speaking of Undine as his wife.

The knight was himself, indeed, just as little pleased with Undine's childish behaviour as the rest; but all his looks and half-reproachful words were to no purpose. It is true, whenever the bride observed the dissatisfaction of her husband—and this occasionally happened—she became more quiet, placed herself beside him, stroked his face with caressing fondness, whispered something smilingly in his ear, and in this manner smoothed the wrinkles that were gathering on his brow. But the moment after, some wild whim would make her resume her antic movements; and all went worse than before.

The priest then spoke in a kind although serious tone: "My fair young maiden, surely no one can look on you without pleasure; but remember betimes so to attune your soul that it may produce a harmony ever in accordance with the soul of your wedded bridegroom."

"SOUL!" cried Undine with a laugh. "What you say has a remarkably pretty sound; and for most people, too, it may be a very instructive and profitable caution. But when a person has no soul at all, how, I pray you, can such attuning be then

69

possible? And this, in truth, is just my condition."

The priest was much hurt, but continued silent in holy displeasure, and turned away his face from the maiden in sorrow. She, however, went up to him with the most winning sweetness, and said:

"Nay, I entreat you first listen to me, before you are angry with me; for your anger is painful to me, and you ought not to give pain to a creature that has not hurt you. Only have patience with me, and I will explain to you every word of what I meant."

It was evident that she had come to say something important; when she suddenly faltered as if seized with inward shuddering, and burst into a passion of tears. They were none of them able to understand the intenseness of her feelings; and, with mingled emotions of fear and anxiety, they gazed on her in silence. Then, wiping away her tears, and looking earnestly at the priest, she at last said:

"There must be something lovely, but at the same time something most awful, about a soul. In the name of God, holy man, were it not better that we never shared a gift so mysterious?"

Again she paused, and restrained her tears, as if waiting for an answer. All in the cottage had risen from their seats, and stepped back from her with horror. She, however, seemed to have eyes for no one but the holy man; an awful curiosity was painted on her features, which appeared terrible to the others.

"Heavily must the soul weigh down its possessor," she pursued, when no one returned her any answer—"very heavily! for already its approaching image overshadows me with anguish and mourning. And, alas, I have till now been so merry and light-hearted!" and she burst into another flood of tears, and covered her face with her veil.

The priest, going up to her with a solemn look, now addressed himself to her, and conjured her, by the name of God most holy, if any spirit of evil possessed her, to remove the light covering from her face. But she sank before him on her knees, and repeated after him every sacred expression he uttered, giving praise to God, and protesting "that she wished well to the whole world."

The priest then spoke to the knight: "Sir bridegroom, I leave you alone with her whom I have united to you in marriage. So far as I can discover, there is nothing of evil in her, but assuredly much that is wonderful. What I recommend to you is—prudence, love, and fidelity."

Thus speaking, he left the apartment; and the fisherman, with his wife, followed him, crossing themselves.

Undine had sunk upon her knees. She uncovered her face, and exclaimed, while she looked fearfully round upon Huldbrand, "Alas! you will now refuse to look upon me as your own; and still I have done nothing evil, poor unhappy child that I am!" She spoke these words with a look so infinitely sweet and touching, that her bridegroom forgot both the confession that had shocked, and the mystery that had perplexed him; and hastening to her, he raised her in his arms. She smiled through her tears; and that smile was like the morning light playing upon a small stream. "You cannot desert me!" she whispered confidingly, and stroked the knight's cheeks with her little soft hands. He turned away from the frightful thoughts that still lurked in the recesses of his soul, and were persuading him that he had been married to a fairy, or some spiteful and mischievous being of the spirit-world. Only the single question, and that almost unawares, escaped from his lips.

"Dearest Undine, tell me this one thing: what was it you meant by 'spirits of earth' and 'Kuhleborn,' when the priest stood knocking at the door?"

"Tales! mere tales of children!" answered Undine, laughing, now quite restored to her wonted gaiety. "I first frightened you with them, and you frightened me. This is the end of the story, and of our nuptial evening."

"Nay, not so," replied the enamoured knight, extinguishing the tapers, and a thousand times kissing his beautiful and beloved bride; while, lighted by the moon that shone brightly through the windows, he bore her into their bridal apartment.

The fresh light of morning woke the young married pair: but Huldbrand lay lost in silent reflection. Whenever, during the night, he had fallen asleep, strange and horrible dreams of spectres had disturbed him; and these shapes, grinning at him by stealth, strove to disguise themselves as beautiful females; and from beautiful females they all at once assumed the appearance of dragons. And when he started up, aroused by the intrusion of these hideous forms, the moonlight shone pale and cold before the windows without. He looked affrighted at Undine, in whose arms he had fallen asleep: and she was reposing in unaltered beauty and sweetness beside him. Then pressing her rosy lips with a light kiss, he again fell into a slumber, only to be awakened by new terrors.

When fully awake, he had thought over this connection. He reproached himself for any doubt that could lead him into error in regard to his lovely wife. He also confessed to her his injustice; but she only gave him her fair hand, sighed deeply, and remained silent. Yet a glance of fervent tenderness, an expression of the soul beaming in her eyes, such as he had never witnessed there before, left him in undoubted assurance that Undine bore him no ill-will.

He then rose joyfully, and leaving her, went to the common apartment, where the inmates of the house had already met. The three were sitting round the hearth with an air of anxiety about them, as if they feared trusting themselves to raise their voice above a low, apprehensive undertone. The priest appeared to be praying in his inmost spirit, with a view to avert some fatal calamity. But when they observed the young husband come forth so cheerful, they dispelled the cloud that remained upon their brows: the old fisherman even began to laugh with the knight till his aged wife herself could not help smiling with great good-humour.

Undine had in the meantime got ready, and now entered

the room; all rose to meet her, but remained fixed in perfect admiration—she was so changed, and yet the same. The priest, with paternal affection beaming from his countenance, first went up to her; and as he raised his hand to pronounce a blessing, the beautiful bride sank on her knees before him with religious awe; she begged his pardon in terms both respectful and submissive for any foolish things she might have uttered the evening before, and entreated him with emotion to pray for the welfare of her soul. She then rose, kissed her foster-parents, and, after thanking them for all the kindness they had shown her, said:

"Oh, I now feel in my inmost heart how much, how infinitely much, you have done for me, you dear, dear friends of my childhood!"

At first she was wholly unable to tear herself away from their affectionate caresses; but the moment she saw the good old mother busy in getting breakfast, she went to the hearth, applied herself to cooking the food and putting it on the table, and would not suffer her to take the least share in the work.

She continued in this frame of spirit the whole day: calm, kind attentive—half matronly, and half girlish. The three who had been longest acquainted with her expected every instant to see her capricious spirit break out in some whimsical change or sportive vagary. But their fears were quite unnecessary. Undine continued as mild and gentle as an angel. The priest found it all but impossible to remove his eyes from her; and he often said to the bridegroom:

"The bounty of Heaven, sir, through me its unworthy instrument, entrusted to you yesterday an invaluable treasure; cherish it as you ought, and it will promote your temporal and eternal welfare."

Toward evening Undine was hanging upon the knight's arm with lowly tenderness, while she drew him gently out before the door, where the setting sun shone richly over the fresh grass, and upon the high, slender boles of the trees. Her emotion was visible: the dew of sadness and love swam in her eyes, while a tender and fearful secret seemed to hover upon her lips, but was only made known by hardly-breathed sighs. She led her husband farther and farther onward without speaking. When he asked her questions, she replied only with looks, in which, it is true, there appeared to be no immediate answer to his inquiries, but a whole heaven of love and timid devotion. Thus they reached the margin of the swollen forest stream, and the knight was astonished to see it gliding away with so gentle a murmuring of its waves, that no vestige of its former swell and wildness was now discernible.

"By morning it will be wholly drained off," said the beautiful wife, almost weeping, "and you will then be able to travel, without anything to hinder you, whithersoever you will."

"Not without you, dear Undine," replied the knight, laughing; "think, only, were I disposed to leave you, both the Church and the spiritual powers, the Emperor and the laws of the realm, would require the fugitive to be seized and restored to you."

"All this depends on you—all depends on you," whispered his little companion, half weeping and half smiling. "But I still feel sure that you will not leave me; I love you too deeply to fear that misery. Now bear me over to that little island which lies before us. There shall the decision be made. I could easily, indeed, glide through that mere rippling of the water without your aid, but it is so sweet to lie in your arms; and should you determine to put me away, I shall have rested in them once more,... for the last time."

Huldbrand was so full of strange anxiety and emotion, that he knew not what answer to make her. He took her in his arms and carried her over, now first realizing the fact that this was the same little island from which he had borne her back to the old fisherman, the first night of his arrival. On the farther side, he placed her upon the soft grass, and was throwing himself lovingly near his beautiful burden; but she said to him, "Not here, but opposite me. I shall read my doom in your eyes, even before your lips pronounce it: now listen attentively to what I shall relate to you." And she began:

"You must know, my own love, that there are beings in the elements which bear the strongest resemblance to the human race, and which, at the same time, but seldom become visible to you. The wonderful salamanders sparkle and sport amid the flames; deep in the earth the meagre and malicious gnomes pursue their revels; the forest-spirits belong to the air, and wander in the woods; while in the seas, rivers, and streams live the widespread race of water-spirits. These last, beneath resounding domes of crystal, through which the sky can shine with its sun and stars, inhabit a region of light and beauty; lofty coral-trees glow with blue and crimson fruits in their gardens; they walk over the pure sand of the sea, among exquisitely variegated shells, and amid whatever of beauty the old world possessed, such as the present is no more worthy to enjoy— creations which the floods covered with their secret veils of silver; and now these noble monuments sparkle below, stately and solemn, and bedewed by the water, which loves them, and calls forth from their crevices delicate moss-flowers and enwreathing tufts of sedge.

"Now the nation that dwell there are very fair and lovely to behold, for the most part more beautiful than human beings. Many a fisherman has been so fortunate as to catch a view of a delicate maiden of the waters, while she was floating and singing upon the deep. He would then spread far the fame of her beauty; and to such wonderful females men are wont to give the name of Undines. But what need of saying more?—You, my dear husband, now actually behold an Undine before you."

The knight would have persuaded himself that his lovely wife was under the influence of one of her odd whims, and that she was only amusing herself and him with her extravagant inventions. He wished it might be so. But with whatever emphasis he said this to himself, he still could not credit the hope for a moment: a strange shivering shot through his soul; unable to utter a word, he gazed upon the sweet speaker with a fixed eye. She shook her head in distress, sighed from her full heart, and then proceeded in the following manner:—"We should be far superior to you, who are another race of the human family,— for we also call ourselves human beings, as we resemble them in form and features—had we not one evil peculiar to ourselves. Both we and the beings I have mentioned as inhabiting the other elements vanish into air at death and go out of existence, spirit and body, so that no vestige of us remains; and when you hereafter awake to a purer state of being, we shall remain where sand, and sparks, and wind, and waves remain. Thus we have no souls; the element moves us, and, again, is obedient to our will, while we live, though it scatters us like dust when we die; and as we have nothing to trouble us, we are as merry as nightingales, little gold-fishes, and other pretty children of nature.

"But all beings aspire to rise in the scale of existence higher than they are. It was therefore the wish of my father, who is a powerful water-prince in the Mediterranean Sea, that his only daughter should become possessed of a soul, although she should have to endure many of the sufferings of those who share that gift.

"Now the race to which I belong have no other means of obtaining a soul than by forming with an individual of your own the most intimate union of love. I am now possessed of a soul, and my soul thanks you, my best beloved, and never shall cease to thank you, if you do not render my whole future life miserable. For what will become of me, if you avoid and reject me? Still, I would not keep you as my own by artifice. And should you decide to cast me off, then do it now, and return alone to the shore. I will plunge into this brook, where my uncle will receive me; my uncle, who here in the forest, far removed from his other friends, passes his strange and solitary existence. But he is powerful, as well as revered and beloved by many great rivers; and as he brought me hither to the fisherman a light-hearted and laughing child, he will take me home to my parents a woman, gifted with a soul, with power to love and to suffer."

She was about to add something more, when Huldbrand, with the most heartfelt tenderness and love, clasped her in his arms, and again bore her back to the shore. There, amid tears and kisses, he first swore never to forsake his affectionate wife, and esteemed himself even more happy than Pygmalion, for whom Venus gave life to his beautiful statue, and thus changed it into a beloved wife. Supported by his arm, and in the confidence of affection, Undine returned to the cottage; and now she first realized with her whole heart how little cause she had for regretting what she had left—the crystal palace of her mysterious father.

CHAPTER V

Next morning, when Huldbrand awoke from slumber, and perceived that his beautiful wife was not by his side, he began to give way again to his wild imaginations—that his marriage, and even the lovely Undine herself, were only shadows without substance—only mere illusions of enchantment. But she entered the door at the same moment, kissed him, seated herself on the bed by his side, and said:

"I have been out somewhat early this morning, to see whether my uncle keeps his word. He has already restored the waters of the flood to his own calm channel, and he now flows through the forest a rivulet as before, in a lonely and dreamlike current. His friends, too, both of the water and the air, have resumed their usual peaceful tenor; all will again proceed with order and tranquillity; and you can travel homeward, without fear of the flood, whenever you choose."

It seemed to the mind of Huldbrand that he must be in some waking dream, so little was he able to understand the nature of his wife's strange relative. Notwithstanding this he made no remark upon what she had told him, and her surpassing loveliness soon lulled every misgiving and discomfort to rest.

Some time afterwards, while he was standing with her before the door, and surveying the verdant point of land, with its boundary of bright waters, such a feeling of bliss came over him in this cradle of his love, that he exclaimed:

"Shall we, then, so early as to-day, begin our journey? Why should we? It is probable that abroad in the world we shall find no days more delightful than those we have spent in this green isle so secret and so secure. Let us yet see the sun go down here two or three times more."

"Just as my lord wills," replied Undine meekly. "Only we must remember, that my foster-parents will, at all events, see me depart with pain; and should they now, for the first time, discover the true soul in me, and how fervently I can now love and honour them, their feeble eyes would surely become blind with weeping. As yet they consider my present quietness and gentleness as of no better promise than they were formerly— like the calm of the lake just while the air remains tranquil— and they will learn soon to cherish a little tree or flower as they have cherished me. Let me not, then, make known to them this newly bestowed, this loving heart, at the very moment they must lose it for this world; and how could I conceal what I have gained, if we continued longer together?"

Huldbrand yielded to her representation, and went to the aged couple to confer with them respecting his journey, on which he proposed to set out that very hour. The priest offered himself as a companion to the young married pair; and, after taking a short farewell, he held the bridle, while the knight lifted his beautiful wife upon his horse; and with rapid steps they crossed the dry channel with her toward the forest. Undine wept in silent but intense emotion; the old people, as she moved away, were more clamorous in the expression of their grief. They appeared to feel, at the moment of separation, all that they were losing in their affectionate foster-daughter.

The three travellers had reached the thickest shades of the forest without interchanging a word. It must have been a fair sight, in that hall of leafy verdure, to see this lovely woman's form sitting on the noble and richly-ornamented steed, on her left hand the venerable priest in the white garb of his order, on her right the blooming young knight, clad in splendid raiment of scarlet, gold, and violet, girt with a sword that flashed in the sun, and attentively walking beside her. Huldbrand had no eyes but for his wife; Undine, who had dried her tears of tenderness, had no eyes but for him; and they soon entered into the still and voiceless converse of looks and gestures, from which, after

79

some time, they were awakened by the low discourse which the priest was holding with a fourth traveller, who had meanwhile joined them unobserved.

He wore a white gown, resembling in form the dress of the priest's order, except that his hood hung very low over his face, and that the whole drapery floated in such wide folds around him as obliged him every moment to gather it up and throw it over his arm, or by some management of this sort to get it out of his way, and still it did not seem in the least to impede his movements. When the young couple became aware of his presence, he was saying:

"And so, venerable sir, many as have been the years I have dwelt here in this forest, I have never received the name of hermit in your sense of the word. For, as I said before, I know nothing of penance, and I think, too, that I have no particular need of it. Do you ask me why I am so attached to the forest? It is because its scenery is so peculiarly picturesque, and affords me so much pastime when, in my floating white garments, I pass through its world of leaves and dusky shadows;—and when a sweet sunbeam glances down upon me at times unexpectedly."

"You are a very singular man," replied the priest, "and I should like to have a more intimate acquaintance with you."

"And who, then, may you be yourself, to pass from one thing to another?" inquired the stranger.

"I am called Father Heilmann," answered the holy man; "and I am from the cloister of Our Lady of the Salutation, beyond the lake."

"Well, well," replied the stranger, "my name is Kuhleborn; and were I a stickler for the nice distinctions of rank, I might, with equal propriety, require you to give me the title of noble lord of Kuhleborn, or free lord of Kuhleborn; for I am as free as the birds in the forest, and, it may be, a trifle more so. For example, I now have something to tell that young lady there." And before they were aware of his purpose, he was on the other side of the priest, close to Undine, and stretching himself high into the air, in order to whisper something in her ear. But she shrank from him in terror, and exclaimed:

"I have nothing more to do with you."

"Ho, ho," cried the stranger with a laugh, "you have made a grand marriage indeed, since you no longer know your own relations! Have you no recollection, then, of your uncle Kuhleborn, who so faithfully bore you on his back to this region?"

"However that may be," replied Undine, "I entreat you never to appear in my presence again. I am now afraid of you; and will not my husband fear and forsake me, if he sees me associate with such strange company and kindred?"

"You must not forget, my little niece," said Kuhleborn, "that I am with you here as a guide; otherwise those madcap spirits of the earth, the gnomes that haunt this forest, would play you some of their mischievous pranks. Let me therefore still accompany you in peace. Even the old priest there had a better recollection of me than you have; for he just now assured me that I seemed to be very familiar to him, and that I must have been with him in the ferry-boat, out of which he tumbled into the waves. He certainly did see me there; for I was no other than the water-spout that tore him out of it, and kept him from sinking, while I safely wafted him ashore to your wedding."

Undine and the knight turned their eyes upon Father Heilmann; but he appeared to be moving forward, just as if he were dreaming or walking in his sleep, and no longer to be conscious of a word that was spoken. Undine then said to Kuhleborn: "I already see yonder the end of the forest. We have no further need of your assistance, and nothing now gives us alarm but yourself. I therefore beseech you, by our mutual love and good-will, to vanish, and allow us to proceed in peace."

Kuhleborn seemed to become angry at this: he darted a frightful look at Undine, and grinned fiercely upon her. She shrieked aloud, and called her husband to protect her. The knight sprang round the horse as quick as lightning, and, brandishing his sword, struck at Kuhleborn's head. But instead of severing it from his body, the sword merely flashed through a torrent, which rushed foaming near them from a lofty cliff; and with a splash, which much resembled in sound a burst of laughter, the stream all at once poured upon them and gave them a thorough wetting. The priest, as if suddenly awakening from a trance, coolly observed: "This is what I have been some time expecting, because the brook has descended from the steep so close beside us—though at first sight, indeed, it appeared to resemble a man, and to possess the power of speech."

As the waterfall came rushing from its crag, it distinctly uttered these words in Huldbrand's ear: "Rash knight! valiant knight! I am not angry with you; I have no quarrel with you; only continue to defend your lovely little wife with the same spirit, you bold knight! you valiant champion!"

After advancing a few steps farther, the travellers came out upon open ground. The imperial city lay bright before them; and the evening sun, which gilded its towers with gold, kindly dried their garments that had been so completely drenched.

The sudden disappearance of the young knight, Huldbrand of Ringstetten, had occasioned much remark in the imperial city, and no small concern amongst those who, as well on account of his expertness in tourney and dance, as of his mild and amiable manners, had become attached to him. His attendants were unwilling to quit the place without their master, although not a soul of them had been courageous enough to follow him into the fearful recesses of the forest. They remained, therefore, at the hostelry, idly hoping, as men are wont to do, and keeping the fate of their lost lord fresh in remembrance by their lamentations.

Now when the violent storms and floods had been observed immediately after his departure, the destruction of the handsome stranger became all but certain; even Bertalda had openly discovered her sorrow, and detested herself for having been the cause of his taking that fatal excursion into the forest.

Her foster-parents, the duke and duchess, had meanwhile come to take her away; but Bertalda persuaded them to remain with her until some certain news of Huldbrand should be obtained, whether he were living or dead. She endeavoured also to prevail upon several young knights, who were assiduous in courting her favour, to go in quest of the noble adventurer in the forest. But she refused to pledge her hand as the reward of the enterprise, because she still cherished, it might be, a hope of its being claimed by the returning knight; and no one would consent, for a glove, a riband, or even a kiss, to expose his life to bring back so very dangerous a rival.

When Huldbrand now made his sudden and unexpected appearance, his attendants, the inhabitants of the city, and almost every one rejoiced. This was not the case with Bertalda; for although it might be quite a welcome event to others that he brought with him a wife of such exquisite loveliness, and Father Heilmann as a witness of their marriage, Bertalda could not but view the affair with grief and vexation. She had, in truth, become attached to the young knight with her whole soul; and her mourning for his absence, or supposed death, had shown this more than she could now have wished.

But notwithstanding all this, she conducted herself like a wise maiden in circumstances of such delicacy, and lived on the most friendly terms with Undine, whom the whole city looked upon as a princess that Huldbrand had rescued in the forest from some evil enchantment. Whenever any one questioned either herself or her husband relative to surmises of this nature, they had wisdom enough to remain silent, or wit enough to evade the inquiries. The lips of Father Heilmann had been sealed in regard to idle gossip of every kind; and besides, on Huldbrand's arrival, he had immediately returned to his cloister: so that people were obliged to rest contented with their own wild conjectures; and even Bertalda herself ascertained nothing more of the truth than others.

For the rest, Undine daily felt more love for the fair maiden.

"We must have been before acquainted with each other," she often used to say to her, "or else there must be some mysterious connection between us, for it is incredible that any one so perfectly without cause—I mean, without some deep and secret cause—should be so fondly attached to another as I have been to you from the first moment of our meeting."

And even Bertalda could not deny that she felt a confiding impulse, an attraction of tenderness toward Undine, much as she deemed this fortunate rival the cause of her bitterest disappointment. Under the influence of this mutual regard, they found means to persuade, the one her foster-parents, and the other her husband, to defer the day of separation to a period more and more remote; nay, more, they had already begun to talk of a plan for Bertalda's accompanying Undine to Castle Ringstetten, near one of the sources of the Danube.

Once on a fine evening they happened to be talking over their scheme just as they passed the high trees that bordered the public walk. The young married pair, though it was somewhat late, had called upon Bertalda to invite her to share their enjoyment; and all three proceeded familiarly up and down beneath the dark blue heaven, not seldom interrupted in their converse by the admiration which they could not but bestow upon the magnificent fountain in the middle of the square, and upon the wonderful rush and shooting upward of its waters. All was sweet and soothing to their minds. Among the shadows of the trees stole in glimmerings of light from the adjacent houses (sic). A low murmur as of children at play, and of other persons who were enjoying their walk, floated around them—they were so alone, and yet sharing so much of social happiness in the bright and stirring world, that whatever had appeared rough by day now became smooth of its own accord. All the three friends could no longer see the slightest cause for hesitation in regard to Bertalda's taking the journey.

At that instant, while they were just fixing the day of their departure, a tall man approached them from the middle of the square, bowed respectfully to the company, and spoke something in the young bride's ear. Though displeased with the interruption and its cause, she walked aside a few steps with the stranger; and both began to whisper, as it seemed, in a foreign tongue. Huldbrand thought he recognized the strange man of the forest, and he gazed upon him so fixedly, that he neither heard nor answered the astonished inquiries of Bertalda. All at once Undine clapped her hands with delight, and turned back from the stranger, laughing: he, frequently shaking his head, retired with a hasty step and discontented air, and descended into the fountain. Huldbrand now felt perfectly certain that his conjecture was correct. But Bertalda asked:

"What, then, dear Undine, did the master of the fountain wish to say to you?"

Undine laughed within herself, and made answer: "The day after to-morrow, my dear child, when the anniversary of your name-day returns, you shall be informed." And this was all she could be prevailed upon to disclose. She merely asked Bertalda to dinner on the appointed day, and requested her to invite her foster-parents; and soon afterwards they separated.

"Kuhleborn?" said Huldbrand to his lovely wife, with an inward shudder when they had taken leave of Bertalda, and were now going home through the darkening streets.

"Yes, it was he," answered Undine; "and he would have wearied me with his foolish warnings. But, in the midst, quite contrary to his intentions, he delighted me with a most welcome piece of news. If you, my dear lord and husband, wish me to acquaint you with it now, you need only command me, and I will freely and from my heart tell you all without reserve. But would you confer upon your Undine a very, very great pleasure, wait till the day after to-morrow, and then you too shall have your share of the surprise."

The knight was quite willing to gratify his wife in what she had asked so sweetly.

And even as she was falling asleep, she murmured to herself, with a smile: "How she will rejoice and be astonished at what her master of the fountain has told me!—dear, dear Bertalda!"

CHAPTER VI

The company were sitting at dinner. Bertalda, adorned with jewels and flowers without number, the presents of her foster-parents and friends, and looking like some goddess of spring, sat beside Undine and Huldbrand at the head of the table. When the sumptuous repast was ended, and the dessert was placed before them, permission was given that the doors should be left open: this was in accordance with the good old custom in Germany, that the common people might see and rejoice in the festivity of their superiors. Among these spectators the servants carried round cake and wine.

Huldbrand and Bertalda waited with secret impatience for the promised explanation, and hardly moved their eyes from Undine. But she still continued silent, and merely smiled to herself with secret and heartfelt satisfaction. All who were made acquainted with the promise she had given could perceive that she was every moment on the point of revealing a happy secret; and yet, as children sometimes delay tasting their choicest dainties, she still withheld the communication. Bertalda and Huldbrand shared the same delightful feeling, while in anxious hope they were expecting the unknown disclosure which they were to receive from the lips of their friend.

At this moment several of the company pressed Undine to sing. This she seemed pleased at; and ordering her lute to be brought, she sang the following words:—

"Morning so bright,
Wild-flowers so gay,
Where high grass so dewy
Crowns the wavy lake's border.

On the meadow's verdant bosom
What glimmers there so white?
Have wreaths of snowy blossoms,
Soft-floating, fallen from heaven?

Ah, see! a tender infant!—
It plays with flowers, unwittingly;
It strives to grasp morn's golden beams.
O where, sweet stranger, where's your home?
Afar from unknown shores
The waves have wafted hither
This helpless little one.

Nay, clasp not, tender darling,
With tiny hand the flowers!
No hand returns the pressure,
The flowers are strange and mute.

They clothe themselves in beauty,
They breathe a rich perfume:
But cannot fold around you
A mother's loving arms;—
Far, far away that mother's fond embrace.

Life's early dawn just opening faint,
Your eye yet beaming heaven's own smile,
So soon your tenderest guardians gone;
Severe, poor child, your fate,—
All, all to you unknown.

A noble duke has crossed the mead,
And near you checked his steed's career:
Wonder and pity touch his heart;
With knowledge high, and manners pure,
He rears you,—makes his castle home your own.

How great, how infinite your gain!
Of all the land you bloom the loveliest;
Yet, ah! the priceless blessing,
The bliss of parents' fondness,
You left on strands unknown!"

Undine let fall her lute with a melancholy smile. The eyes of
Bertalda's noble foster-parents were filled with tears.

"Ah yes, it was so—such was the morning on which I found
you, poor orphan!" cried the duke, with deep emotion; "the
beautiful singer is certainly right: still

'The priceless blessing,
The bliss of parents' fondness,'

it was beyond our power to give you."

"But we must hear, also, what happened to the poor parents,"
said Undine, as she struck the chords, and sung:—

"Through her chambers roams the mother
Searching, searching everywhere;
Seeks, and knows not what, with yearning,
Childless house still finding there.

Childless house!—O sound of anguish!
She alone the anguish knows,
There by day who led her dear one,
There who rocked its night-repose.

Beechen buds again are swelling,
Sunshine warms again the shore;
Ah, fond mother, cease your searching!
Comes the loved and lost no more.

Then when airs of eve are fresh'ning,
　　Home the father wends his way,
While with smiles his woe he's veiling,
　　Gushing tears his heart betray.

Well he knows, within his dwelling,
　　Still as death he'll find the gloom,
Only hear the mother moaning,—
　　No sweet babe to SMILE him home."

"O, tell me, in the name of Heaven tell me, Undine, where are my parents?" cried the weeping Bertalda. "You certainly know; you must have discovered them, you wonderful being; for, otherwise you would never have thus torn my heart. Can they be already here? May I believe it possible?" Her eye glanced rapidly over the brilliant company, and rested upon a lady of high rank who was sitting next to her foster-father.

Then, bending her head, Undine beckoned toward the door, while her eyes overflowed with the sweetest emotion. "Where, then, are the poor parents waiting?" she asked; and the old fisherman, hesitating, advanced with his wife from the crowd of spectators. They looked inquiringly, now at Undine, and now at the beautiful lady who was said to be their daughter.

"It is she! it is she there before you!" exclaimed the restorer of their child, her voice half choked with rapture. And both the aged parents embraced their recovered daughter, weeping aloud and praising God.

But, terrified and indignant, Bertalda tore herself from their arms. Such a discovery was too much for her proud spirit to bear, especially at the moment when she had doubtless expected to see her former splendour increased, and when hope was picturing to her nothing less brilliant than a royal canopy and a crown. It seemed to her as if her rival had contrived all this on purpose to humble her before Huldbrand and the whole world. She reproached Undine; she reviled the old people; and even such offensive words as "deceiver, bribed and perjured impostors," burst from her lips.

The aged wife of the fisherman then said to herself, in a low voice: "Ah, my God, she has become wicked! and yet I feel in my heart that she is my child."

The old fisherman had meanwhile folded his hands, and offered up a silent prayer that she might NOT be his daughter.

Undine, faint and pale as death, turned from the parents to Bertalda, from Bertalda to the parents. She was suddenly cast dawn from all that heaven of happiness in which she had been dreaming, and plunged into an agony of terror and disappointment, which she had never known even in dreams.

"Have you, then, a soul? Have you indeed a soul, Bertalda?" she cried again and again to her angry friend, as if with vehement effort she would arouse her from a sudden delirium or some distracting dream of night, and restore her to recollection.

But when Bertalda became every moment only more and more enraged—when the disappointed parents began to weep aloud—and the company, with much warmth of dispute, were espousing opposite sides—she begged, with such earnestness and dignity, for the liberty of speaking in this her husband's hall, that all around her were in an instant hushed to silence. She then advanced to the upper end of the table, where, both humbled and haughty, Bertalda had seated herself, and, while every eye was fastened upon her, spoke in the following manner:—

"My friends, you appear dissatisfied and disturbed; and you are interrupting, with your strife, a festivity I had hoped would bring joy to you and to me. Ah! I knew nothing of your heartless ways of thinking; and never shall understand them: I am not to blame for the mischief this disclosure has done. Believe me, little as you may imagine this to be the case, it is wholly owing to yourselves. One word more, therefore, is all I have to add; but this is one that must be spoken:—I have uttered nothing but truth. Of the certainty of the fact, I give you the strongest assurance. No other proof can I or will I produce, but this I will affirm in the presence of God. The person who gave me this information was the very same who decoyed the infant Bertalda into the water, and who, after thus taking her from her parents, placed her on the green grass of the meadow, where he knew the duke was to pass."

"She is an enchantress!" cried Bertalda; "a witch, that has intercourse with evil spirits. She acknowledges it herself."

"Never! I deny it!" replied Undine, while a whole heaven of innocence and truth beamed from her eyes. "I am no witch; look upon me, and say if I am."

"Then she utters both falsehood and folly," cried Bertalda; "and she is unable to prove that I am the child of these low people. My noble parents, I entreat you to take me from this company, and out of this city, where they do nothing but shame me."

But the aged duke, a man of honourable feeling, remained unmoved; and his wife remarked:

"We must thoroughly examine into this matter. God forbid that we should move a step from this hall before we do so."

Then the aged wife of the fisherman drew near, made a low obeisance to the duchess and said: "Noble and pious lady, you have opened my heart. Permit me to tell you, that if this evil-disposed maiden is my daughter, she has a mark like a violet between her shoulders, and another of the same kind on the instep of her left foot. If she will only consent to go out of the hall with me—"

"I will not consent to uncover myself before the peasant woman," interrupted Bertalda, haughtily turning her back upon her.

"But before me you certainly will," replied the duchess gravely. "You will follow me into that room, maiden; and the old woman shall go with us."

The three disappeared, and the rest continued where they were, in breathless expectation. In a few minutes the females returned—Bertalda pale as death; and the duchess said: "Justice must be done; I therefore declare that our lady hostess has spoken exact truth. Bertalda is the fisherman's daughter; no further proof is required; and this is all of which, on the present occasion, you need to be informed."

The princely pair went out with their adopted daughter; the fisherman, at a sign from the duke, followed them with his wife. The other guests retired in silence, or suppressing their murmurs; while Undine sank weeping into the arms of Huldbrand.

The lord of Ringstetten would certainly have been more gratified, had the events of this day been different; but even such as they now were, he could by no means look upon them as unwelcome, since his lovely wife had shown herself so full of goodness, sweetness, and kindliness.

"If I have given her a soul," he could not help saying to himself, "I have assuredly given her a better one than my own;" and now he only thought of soothing and comforting his weeping wife, and of removing her even so early as the morrow from a place which, after this cross accident, could not fail to be distasteful to her. Yet it is certain that the opinion of the public concerning her was not changed. As something extraordinary had long before been expected of her, the mysterious discovery of Bertalda's parentage had occasioned little or no surprise; and every one who became acquainted with Bertalda's story, and with the violence of her behaviour on that occasion, was only disgusted and set against her. Of this state of things, however, the knight and his lady were as yet ignorant; besides, whether the public condemned Bertalda or herself, the one view of the affair would have been as distressing to Undine as the other; and thus they came to the conclusion that the wisest course they could take, was to leave behind them the walls of the old city with all the speed in their power.

With the earliest beams of morning, a brilliant carriage for Undine drove up to the door of the inn; the horses of Huldbrand and his attendants stood near, stamping the pavement, impatient to proceed. The knight was leading his beautiful wife from the door, when a fisher-girl came up and met them in the way.

"We have no need of your fish," said Huldbrand, accosting her; "we are this moment setting out on a journey."

Upon this the fisher-girl began to weep bitterly; and then it was that the young couple first perceived it was Bertalda. They immediately returned with her to their apartment, when she informed them that, owing to her unfeeling and violent conduct of the preceding day, the duke and duchess had been so displeased with her, as entirely to withdraw from her their protection, though not before giving her a generous portion. The fisherman, too, had received a handsome gift, and had, the evening before, set out with his wife for his peninsula.

"I would have gone with them," she pursued, "but the old fisherman, who is said to be my father—"

"He is, in truth, your father, Bertalda," said Undine, interrupting her. "See, the stranger whom you took for the master of the water-works gave me all the particulars. He wished to dissuade me from taking you with me to Castle Ringstetten, and therefore disclosed to me the whole mystery."

"Well then," continued Bertalda, "my father—if it must needs be so—my father said: 'I will not take you with me until you are changed. If you will venture to come to us alone through the ill-omened forest, that shall be a proof of your having some regard for us. But come not to me as a lady; come merely as a fisher-girl.' I do as he bade me, for since I am abandoned by all the world, I will live and die in solitude, a poor fisher-girl, with parents equally poor. The forest, indeed, appears very terrible to me. Horrible spectres make it their haunt, and I am so fearful. But how can I help it? I have only come here at this early hour to beg the noble lady of Ringstetten to pardon my unbecoming behaviour of yesterday. Sweet lady, I have the fullest persuasion that you meant to do me a kindness, but you were not aware how severely you would wound me; and then, in my agony and surprise, so many rash and frantic expressions burst from my lips. Forgive me, ah, forgive me! I am in truth so unhappy, already. Only consider what I was but yesterday morning, what I was even at the beginning of your yesterday's festival, and what I am to-day!"

Her words now became inarticulate, lost in a passionate flow of tears, while Undine, bitterly weeping with her, fell upon her neck. So powerful was her emotion, that it was a long time before she could utter a word. At length she said:

"You shall still go with us to Ringstetten; all shall remain just as we lately arranged it; but say 'thou' to me again, and do not call me 'noble lady' any more. Consider, we were changed for each other when we were children; even then we were united by a like fate, and we will strengthen this union with such close affection as no human power shall dissolve. Only first of all you must go with us to Ringstetten. How we shall share all things as sisters, we can talk of after we arrive."

Bertalda looked up to Huldbrand with timid inquiry. He pitied her in her affliction, took her hand, and begged her tenderly to entrust herself to him and his wife.

"We will send a message to your parents," continued he, "giving them the reason why you have not come;"—and he would have added more about his worthy friends of the peninsula, when, perceiving that Bertalda shrank in distress at the mention of them, he refrained. He took her under the arm, lifted her first into the carriage, then Undine, and was soon riding blithely beside them; so persevering was he, too, in urging forward their driver, that in a short time they had left behind them the limits of the city, and a crowd of painful recollections; and now the ladies could take delight in the beautiful country which their progress was continually presenting.

After a journey of some days, they arrived, on a fine evening, at Castle Ringstetten. The young knight being much engaged with the overseers and menials of his establishment, Undine and Bertalda were left alone. They took a walk upon the high rampart of the fortress, and were charmed with the delightful landscape which the fertile Suabia spread around them. While they were viewing the scene, a tall man drew near, who greeted them with respectful civility, and who seemed to Bertalda much to resemble the director of the city fountain. Still less was the resemblance to be mistaken, when Undine, indignant at his intrusion, waved him off with an air of menace; while he, shaking his head, retreated with rapid strides, as he had formerly done, then glided among the trees of a neighbouring grove and disappeared.

"Do not be terrified, Bertalda," said Undine; "the hateful master of the fountain shall do you no harm this time." And then she related to her the particulars of her history, and who she was herself—how Bertalda had been taken away from the people of the peninsula, and Undine left in her place. This relation at first filled the young maiden with amazement and alarm; she imagined her friend must be seized with a sudden madness. But from the consistency of her story, she became more and more convinced that all was true, it so well agreed with former occurrences, and still more convinced from that inward feeling with which truth never fails to make itself known to us. She could not but view it as an extraordinary circumstance that she was herself now living, as it were, in the midst of one of those wild tales which she had formerly heard related. She gazed upon Undine with reverence, but could not keep from a shuddering feeling which seemed to come between her and her friend; and she could not but wonder when the knight, at their evening repast, showed himself so kind and full of love towards a being who appeared to her, after the discoveries just made, more to resemble a phantom of the spirit-world than one of the human race.

CHAPTER VII

The writer of this tale, both because it moves his own heart and he wishes it to move that of others, asks a favour of you, dear reader. Forgive him if he passes over a considerable space of time in a few words, and only tells you generally what therein happened. He knows well that it might be unfolded skilfully, and step by step, how Huldbrand's heart began to turn from Undine and towards Bertalda—how Bertalda met the young knight with ardent love, and how they both looked upon the poor wife as a mysterious being, more to be dreaded than pitied—how Undine wept, and her tears stung the conscience of her husband, without recalling his former love; so that though at times he showed kindness to her, a cold shudder soon forced him to turn from her to his fellow-mortal Bertalda;—all this, the writer knows, might have been drawn out fully, and perhaps it ought to have been. But it would have made him too sad; for he has witnessed such things, and shrinks from recalling even their shadow. Thou knowest, probably, the like feeling, dear reader; for it is the lot of mortal man. Happy art thou if thou hast received the injury, not inflicted it; for in this case it is more blessed to receive than to give. Then only a soft sorrow at such a recollection passes through thy heart, and perhaps a quiet tear trickles down thy cheek over the faded flowers in which thou once so heartily rejoiced. This is enough: we will not pierce our hearts with a thousand separate stings, but only bear in mind that all happened as I just now said.

Poor Undine was greatly troubled; and the other two were very far from being happy. Bertalda in particular, whenever she was in the slightest degree opposed in her wishes, attributed the cause to the jealousy and oppression of the injured wife. She was therefore daily in the habit of showing a haughty and imperious demeanour, to which Undine yielded with a sad submission; and which was generally encouraged strongly by the now blinded Huldbrand.

What disturbed the inmates of the castle still more, was the endless variety of wonderful apparitions which assailed Huldbrand and Bertalda in the vaulted passages of the building, and of which nothing had ever been heard before within the memory of man. The tall white man, in whom Huldbrand but too plainly recognized Undine's uncle Kuhleborn, and Bertalda the spectral master of the waterworks, often passed before them with threatening aspect and gestures; more especially, however, before Bertalda, so that, through terror, she had several times already fallen sick, and had, in consequence, frequently thought of quitting the castle. Yet partly because Huldbrand was but too dear to her, and she trusted to her innocence, since no words of love had passed between them, and partly also because she knew not whither to direct her steps, she lingered where she was.

The old fisherman, on receiving the message from the lord of Ringstetten that Bertalda was his guest, returned answer in some lines almost too illegible to be deciphered, but still the best his advanced life and long disuse of writing permitted him to form.

"I have now become," he wrote, "a poor old widower, for my beloved and faithful wife is dead. But lonely as I now sit in my cottage, I prefer Bertalda's remaining where she is, to her living with me. Only let her do nothing to hurt my dear Undine, else she will have my curse."

The last words of this letter Bertalda flung to the winds; but the permission to remain from home, which her father had granted her, she remembered and clung to—just as we are all of us wont to do in similar circumstances.

One day, a few moments after Huldbrand had ridden out, Undine called together the domestics of the family, and ordered them to bring a large stone, and carefully to cover with it a magnificent fountain, that was situated in the middle of the castle court. The servants objected that it would oblige them to bring water from the valley below. Undine smiled sadly.

"I am sorry, my friends," replied she, "to increase your labour; I would rather bring up the water-vessels myself: but this fountain must indeed be closed. Believe me when I say that it must be done, and that only by doing it we can avoid a greater evil."

The domestics were all rejoiced to gratify their gentle mistress; and making no further inquiry, they seized the enormous stone. While they were raising it in their hands, and were now on the point of adjusting it over the fountain, Bertalda came running to the place, and cried, with an air of command, that they must stop; that the water she used, so improving to her complexion, was brought from this fountain, and that she would by no means allow it to be closed.

This time, however, Undine, while she showed her usual gentleness, showed more than her usual resolution: she said it belonged to her, as mistress of the house, to direct the household according to her best judgment; and that she was accountable in this to no one but her lord and husband.

"See, O pray see," exclaimed the dissatisfied and indignant Bertalda, "how the beautiful water is curling and curving, winding and waving there, as if disturbed at being shut out from the bright sunshine, and from the cheerful view of the human countenance, for whose mirror it was created."

In truth the water of the fountain was agitated, and foaming and hissing in a surprising manner; it seemed as if there were something within possessing life and will, that was struggling to free itself from confinement. But Undine only the more earnestly urged the accomplishment of her commands. This earnestness was scarcely required. The servants of the castle were as happy in obeying their gentle lady, as in opposing the haughty spirit of Bertalda; and however the latter might scold and threaten, still the stone was in a few minutes lying firm over the opening of the fountain. Undine leaned thoughtfully over it, and wrote with her beautiful fingers on the flat surface. She must, however, have had something very sharp and corrosive in her hand, for when she retired, and the domestics went up to examine the stone, they discovered various strange characters upon it, which none of them had seen there before.

When the knight returned home, toward evening, Bertalda received him with tears, and complaints of Undine's conduct. He cast a severe glance of reproach at his poor wife, and she looked down in distress; yet she said very calmly:

"My lord and husband, you never reprove even a bondslave before you hear his defence; how much less, then, your wedded wife!"

"Speak! what moved you to this singular conduct?" said the knight with a gloomy countenance.

"I could wish to tell you when we are entirely alone," said Undine, with a sigh.

"You can tell me equally well in the presence of Bertalda," he replied.

"Yes, if you command me," said Undine; "but do not command me—pray, pray do not!"

She looked so humble, affectionate, and obedient, that the heart of the knight was touched and softened, as if it felt the influence of a ray from better times. He kindly took her arm within his, and led her to his apartment, where she spoke as follows:

"You already know something, my beloved lord, of Kuhleborn, my evil-disposed uncle, and have often felt displeasure at meeting him in the passages of this castle. Several times has he terrified Bertalda even to swooning. He does this because he possesses no soul, being a mere elemental mirror of the outward world, while of the world within he can give no reflection. Then, too, he sometimes observes that you are displeased with me, that in my childish weakness I weep at this, and that Bertalda, it may be, laughs at the same moment. Hence it is that he imagines all is wrong with us, and in various ways mixes with our circle unbidden. What do I gain by reproving him, by showing displeasure, and sending him away? He does not believe a word I say. His poor nature has no idea that the joys and sorrows of love have so sweet a resemblance, and are so intimately connected that no power on earth is able to separate them. A smile shines in the midst of tears, and a smile calls forth tears from their dwelling-place."

She looked up at Huldbrand, smiling and weeping, and he again felt within his heart all the magic of his former love. She perceived it, and pressed him more tenderly to her, while with tears of joy she went on thus:

"When the disturber of our peace would not be dismissed with words, I was obliged to shut the door upon him; and the only entrance by which he has access to us is that fountain. His connection with the other water-spirits here in this region is cut off by the valleys that border upon us; and his kingdom first commences farther off on the Danube, in whose tributary streams some of his good friends have their abode. For this reason I caused the stone to be placed over the opening of the fountain, and inscribed characters upon it, which baffle all the efforts of my suspicious uncle; so that he now has no power of intruding either upon you or me, or Bertalda. Human beings, it is true, notwithstanding the characters I have inscribed there, are able to raise the stone without any extraordinary trouble; there is nothing to prevent them. If you choose, therefore, remove it, according to Bertalda's desire; but she assuredly knows not what she asks. The rude Kuhleborn looks with peculiar ill-will upon her; and should those things come to pass that he has predicted to me, and which may happen without your meaning any evil, ah! dearest, even you yourself would be exposed to peril."

Huldbrand felt the generosity of his gentle wife in the depth of his heart, since she had been so active in confining her formidable defender, and even at the very moment she was reproached for it by Bertalda. He pressed her in his arms with

101

the tenderest affection, and said with emotion:

"The stone shall remain unmoved; all remains, and ever shall remain, just as you choose to have it, my sweetest Undine!"

At these long-withheld expressions of tenderness, she returned his caresses with lowly delight, and at length said:

"My dearest husband, since you are so kind and indulgent to-day, may I venture to ask a favour of you? See now, it is with you as with summer. Even amid its highest splendour, summer puts on the flaming and thundering crown of glorious tempests, in which it strongly resembles a king and god on earth. You, too, are sometimes terrible in your rebukes; your eyes flash lightning, while thunder resounds in your voice; and although this may be quite becoming to you, I in my folly cannot but sometimes weep at it. But never, I entreat you, behave thus toward me on a river, or even when we are near any water. For if you should, my relations would acquire a right over me. They would inexorably tear me from you in their fury, because they would conceive that one of their race was injured; and I should be compelled, as long as I lived, to dwell below in the crystal palaces, and never dare to ascend to you again; or should THEY SEND me up to you!—O God! that would be far worse still. No, no, my beloved husband; let it not come to that, if your poor Undine is dear to you."

He solemnly promised to do as she desired, and, inexpressibly happy and full of affection, the married pair returned from the apartment. At this very moment Bertalda came with some work-people whom she had meanwhile ordered to attend her, and said with a fretful air, which she had assumed of late:

"Well, now the secret consultation is at an end, the stone may be removed. Go out, workmen, and see to it."

The knight, however, highly resenting her impertinence, said, in brief and very decisive terms: "The stone remains where it is!" He reproved Bertalda also for the vehemence that she had shown towards his wife. Whereupon the workmen, smiling with secret satisfaction, withdrew; while Bertalda, pale with rage, hurried away to her room.

When the hour of supper came, Bertalda was waited for in vain. They sent for her; but the domestic found her apartments empty, and brought back with him only a sealed letter, addressed to the knight. He opened it in alarm, and read:

"I feel with shame that I am only the daughter of a poor fisherman. That I for one moment forgot this, I will make expiation in the miserable hut of my parents. Farewell to you and your beautiful wife!"

Undine was troubled at heart. With eagerness she entreated Huldbrand to hasten after their friend, who had flown, and bring her back with him. Alas! she had no occasion to urge him. His passion for Bertalda again burst forth with vehemence. He hurried round the castle, inquiring whether any one had seen which way the fair fugitive had gone. He could gain no information; and was already in the court on his horse, determining to take at a venture the road by which he had conducted Bertalda to the castle, when there appeared a page, who assured him that he had met the lady on the path to the Black Valley. Swift as an arrow, the knight sprang through the gate in the direction pointed out, without hearing Undine's voice of agony, as she cried after him from the window:

"To the Black Valley? Oh, not there! Huldbrand, not there! Or if you will go, for Heaven's sake take me with you!"

But when she perceived that all her calling was of no avail, she ordered her white palfrey to be instantly saddled, and followed the knight, without permitting a single servant to accompany her.

The Black Valley lies secluded far among the mountains. What its present name may be I am unable to say. At the time of which I am speaking, the country-people gave it this appellation from the deep obscurity produced by the shadows of lofty trees, more especially by a crowded growth of firs that covered this region of moorland. Even the brook, which bubbled between the rocks, assumed the same dark hue, and showed nothing of that cheerful aspect which streams are wont to wear that have the blue sky immediately over them.

It was now the dusk of evening; and between the heights it had become extremely wild and gloomy. The knight, in great anxiety, skirted the border of the brook. He was at one time fearful that, by delay, he should allow the fugitive to advance too far before him; and then again, in his too eager rapidity, he was afraid he might somewhere overlook and pass by her, should she be desirous of concealing herself from his search. He had in the meantime penetrated pretty far into the valley, and might hope soon to overtake the maiden, provided he were pursuing the right track. The fear, indeed, that he might not as yet have gained it, made his heart beat with more and more of anxiety. In the stormy night which was now approaching, and which always fell more fearfully over this valley, where would the delicate Bertalda shelter herself, should he fail to find her? At last, while these thoughts were darting across his mind, he saw something white glimmer through the branches on the ascent of the mountain. He thought he recognized Bertalda's robe; and he directed his course towards it. But his horse refused to go forward; he reared with a fury so uncontrollable, and his master was so unwilling to lose a moment, that (especially as he saw the thickets were altogether impassable on horseback) he dismounted, and, having fastened his snorting steed to an elm, worked his way with caution through the matted underwood. The branches, moistened by the cold drops of the evening dew, struck against his forehead and cheeks; distant thunder muttered from the further side of the mountains; and everything put on so strange an appearance, that he began to feel a dread of the white figure, which now lay at a short distance from him upon the ground. Still, he could see distinctly that it was a female, either asleep or in a swoon, and dressed in long white garments such as Bertalda had worn the past day. Approaching quite near to her, he made a rustling with the branches and a ringing with his sword; but she did not move.

"Bertalda!" he cried, at first low, then louder and louder; yet she heard him not. At last, when he uttered the dear name with an energy yet more powerful, a hollow echo from the mountain-summits around the valley returned the deadened sound, "Bertalda!" Still the sleeper continued insensible. He stooped down; but the duskiness of the valley, and the obscurity of twilight would not allow him to distinguish her features. While, with painful uncertainty, he was bending over her, a flash of lightning suddenly shot across the valley. By this stream of light he saw a frightfully distorted visage close to his own, and a hoarse voice reached his ear:

"You enamoured swain, give me a kiss!" Huldbrand sprang upon his feet with a cry of horror, and the hideous figure rose with him.

"Go home!" it cried, with a deep murmur: "the fiends are abroad. Go home! or I have you!" And it stretched towards him its long white arms.

"Malicious Kuhleborn!" exclaimed the knight, with restored energy; "if Kuhleborn you are, what business have you here?—what's your will, you goblin? There, take your kiss!" And in fury he struck his sword at the form. But it vanished like vapour; and a rush of water, which wetted him through and through, left him in no doubt with what foe he had been engaged.

"He wishes to frighten me back from my pursuit of Bertalda," said he to himself. "He imagines that I shall be terrified at his senseless tricks, and resign the poor distressed maiden to his power, so that he can wreak his vengeance upon her at will. But that he shall not, weak spirit of the flood! What the heart of man can do, when it exerts the full force of its will and of its noblest powers, the poor goblin cannot fathom."

He felt the truth of his words, and that they had inspired his heart with fresh courage. Fortune, too, appeared to favour him; for, before reaching his fastened steed, he distinctly heard the voice of Bertalda, weeping not far before him, amid the roar of the thunder and the tempest, which every moment increased. He flew swiftly towards the sound, and found the trembling maiden, just as she was attempting to climb the steep, hoping to escape from the dreadful darkness of this valley. He drew near her with expressions of love; and bold and proud as her resolution had so lately been, she now felt nothing but joy that the man whom she so passionately loved should rescue her from this frightful solitude, and thus call her back to the joyful life in the castle. She followed almost unresisting, but so spent with fatigue, that the knight was glad to bring her to his horse, which he now hastily unfastened from the elm, in order to lift the fair wanderer upon him, and then to lead him carefully by the reins through the uncertain shades of the valley.

But, owing to the wild apparition of Kuhleborn, the horse had become wholly unmanageable. Rearing and wildly snorting as he was, the knight must have used uncommon effort to mount the beast himself; to place the trembling Bertalda upon him was impossible. They were compelled, therefore, to return home on foot. While with one hand the knight drew the steed after him by the bridle, he supported the tottering Bertalda with the other. She exerted all the strengths in her power in order to escape speedily from this vale of terrors. But weariness weighed her down like lead; and all her limbs trembled, partly in consequence of what she had suffered from the extreme terror which Kuhleborn had already caused her, and partly from her present fear at the roar of the tempest and thunder amid the mountain forest.

At last she slid from the arm of the knight; and sinking upon the moss, she said: "Only let me lie here, my noble lord. I suffer the punishment due to my folly; and I must perish here through faintness and dismay."

"Never, gentle lady, will I leave you," cried Huldbrand, vainly trying to restrain the furious animal he was leading, for the horse was all in a foam, and began to chafe more ungovernably than before, till the knight was glad to keep him at such a distance from the exhausted maiden as to save her from a new alarm. But hardly had he withdrawn five steps with the frantic steed when she began to call after him in the most sorrowful accents, fearful that he would actually leave her in this horrible wilderness. He was at a loss what course to take. He would gladly have given the enraged beast his liberty; he would have let him rush away amid the night and exhaust his fury, had he not feared that in this narrow defile his iron-shod hoofs might come thundering over the very spot where Bertalda lay.

In this extreme peril and embarrassment he heard with delight the rumbling wheels of a waggon as it came slowly descending the stony way behind them. He called out for help; answer was returned in the deep voice of a man, bidding them have patience, but promising assistance; and two grey horses soon after shone through the bushes, and near them their driver in the white frock of a carter; and next appeared a great sheet of white linen, with which the goods he seemed to be conveying were covered. The greys, in obedience to a shout from their master, stood still. He came up to the knight, and aided him in checking the fury of the foaming charger.

"I know well enough," said he, "what is the matter with the brute. The first time I travelled this way my horses were just as wilful and headstrong as yours. The reason is, there is a water-spirit haunts this valley—and a wicked wight they say he is—who takes delight in mischief and witcheries of this sort. But I have learned a charm; and if you will let me whisper it in your horse's ear, he will stand just as quiet as my silver greys there."

"Try your luck, then, and help us as quickly as possible!" said the impatient knight.

Upon this the waggoner drew down the head of the rearing courser close to his own, and spoke some words in his ear. The animal instantly stood still and subdued; only his quick panting and smoking sweat showed his recent violence.

Huldbrand had little time to inquire by what means this had been effected. He agreed with the man that he should take Bertalda in his waggon, where, as he said, a quantity of soft cotton was stowed, and he might in this way convey her to Castle

Ringstetten. The knight could accompany them on horseback. But the horse appeared to be too much exhausted to carry his master so far. Seeing this, the man advised him to mount the waggon with Bertalda. The horse could be attached to it behind.

"It is down-hill," said he, "and the load for my greys will therefore be light."

The knight accepted his offer, and entered the waggon with Bertalda. The horse followed patiently after, while the waggoner, sturdy and attentive, walked beside them.

Amid the silence and deepening obscurity of the night, the tempest sounding more and more remote, in the comfortable feeling of their security, a confidential conversation arose between Huldbrand and Bertalda. He reproached her in the most flattering words for her resentful flight. She excused herself with humility and feeling; and from every tone of her voice it shone out, like a lamp guiding to the beloved through night and darkness, that Huldbrand was still dear to her. The knight felt the sense of her words rather than heard the words themselves, and answered simply to this sense.

Then the waggoner suddenly shouted, with a startling voice: "Up, my greys, up with your feet! Hey, now together!—show your spirit!—remember who you are!"

The knight bent over the side of the waggon, and saw that the horses had stepped into the midst of a foaming stream, and were, indeed, almost swimming, while the wheels of the waggon were rushing round and flashing like mill-wheels; and the waggoner had got on before, to avoid the swell of the flood.

"What sort of a road is this? It leads into the middle of the stream!" cried Huldbrand to his guide.

"Not at all, sir," returned he, with a laugh; "it is just the contrary. The stream is running in the middle of our road. Only look about you, and see how all is overflowed!"

The whole valley, in fact, was in commotion, as the waters, suddenly raised and visibly rising, swept over it.

"It is Kuhleborn, that evil water-spirit, who wishes to drown us!" exclaimed the knight. "Have you no charm of protection against him, friend?"

"I have one," answered the waggoner; "but I cannot and must not make use of it before you know who I am."

"Is this a time for riddles?" cried the knight. "The flood is every moment rising higher; and what does it concern ME to know who YOU are?"

"But mayhap it does concern you, though," said the guide; "for I am Kuhleborn."

Thus speaking he thrust his head into the waggon, and laughed with a distorted visage. But the waggon remained a waggon no longer; the grey horses were horses no longer; all was transformed to foam—all sank into the waters that rushed and hissed around them; while the waggoner himself, rising in the form of a gigantic wave, dragged the vainly-struggling courser under the waters, then rose again huge as a liquid tower, swept over the heads of the floating pair, and was on the point of burying them irrecoverably beneath it. Then the soft voice of Undine was heard through the uproar; the moon emerged from the clouds; and by its light Undine was seen on the heights above the valley. She rebuked, she threatened the floods below her. The menacing and tower-like billow vanished, muttering and murmuring; the waters gently flowed away under the beams of the moon; while Undine, like a hovering white dove, flew down from the hill, raised the knight and Bertalda, and bore them to a green spot, where, by her earnest efforts, she soon restored them and dispelled their terrors. She then assisted Bertalda to mount the white palfrey on which she had herself been borne to the valley; and thus all three returned homeward to Castle Ringstetten.

CHAPTER VIII

After this last adventure they lived at the castle undisturbed and in peaceful enjoyment. The knight was more and more impressed with the heavenly goodness of his wife, which she had so nobly shown by her instant pursuit and by the rescue she had effected in the Black Valley, where the power of Kuhleborn again commenced. Undine herself enjoyed that peace and security which never fails the soul as long as it knows distinctly that it is on the right path; and besides, in the newly-awakened love and regard of her husband, a thousand gleams of hope and joy shone upon her.

Bertalda, on the other hand, showed herself grateful, humble, and timid, without taking to herself any merit for so doing. Whenever Huldbrand or Undine began to explain to her their reasons for covering the fountain, or their adventures in the Black Valley, she would earnestly entreat them to spare her the recital, for the recollection of the fountain occasioned her too much shame, and that of the Black Valley too much terror. She learnt nothing more about either of them; and what would she have gained from more knowledge? Peace and joy had visibly taken up their abode at Castle Ringstetten. They enjoyed their present blessings in perfect security, and now imagined that life could produce nothing but pleasant flowers and fruits.

In this happiness winter came and passed away; and spring, with its foliage of tender green, and its heaven of softest blue, succeeded to gladden the hearts of the three inmates of the castle. The season was in harmony with their minds, and their minds imparted their own hues to the season. What wonder, then, that its storks and swallows inspired them also with a disposition to travel? On a bright morning, while they

110

were wandering down to one of the sources of the Danube, Huldbrand spoke of the magnificence of this noble stream, how it continued swelling as it flowed through countries enriched by its waters, with what splendour Vienna rose and sparkled on its banks, and how it grew lovelier and more imposing throughout its progress.

"It must be glorious to trace its course down to Vienna!" Bertalda exclaimed, with warmth; but immediately resuming the humble and modest demeanour she had recently shown, she paused and blushed in silence.

This much moved Undine; and with the liveliest wish to gratify her friend, she said, "What hinders our taking this little voyage?"

Bertalda leapt up with delight, and the two friends at the same moment began painting this enchanting voyage on the Danube in the most brilliant colours. Huldbrand, too, agreed to the project with pleasure; only he once whispered, with something of alarm, in Undine's ear—

"But at that distance Kuhleborn becomes possessed of his power again!"

"Let him come, let him come," she answered with a laugh; "I shall be there, and he dares do none of his mischief in my presence."

Thus was the last impediment removed. They prepared for the expedition, and soon set out upon it with lively spirits and the brightest hopes.

But be not surprised, O man, if events almost always happen very differently from what you expect. That malicious power which lies in ambush for our destruction delights to lull its chosen victim asleep with sweet songs and golden delusions; while, on the other hand, the messenger of heaven often strikes sharply at our door, to alarm and awaken us.

During the first days of their passage down the Danube they were unusually happy. The further they advanced upon the waters of this proud river, the views became more and more fair. But amid scenes otherwise most delicious, and from which they had promised themselves the purest delight, the stubborn Kuhleborn, dropping all disguise, began to show his power of annoying them. He had no other means of doing this, indeed, than by tricks—for Undine often rebuked the swelling waves or the contrary winds, and then the insolence of the enemy was instantly humbled and subdued; but his attacks were renewed, and Undine's reproofs again became necessary, so that the pleasure of the fellow-travellers was completely destroyed. The boatmen, too, were continually whispering to one another in dismay, and eying their three superiors with distrust, while even the servants began more and more to form dismal surmises, and to watch their master and mistress with looks of suspicion.

Huldbrand often said in his own mind, "This comes when like marries not like—when a man forms an unnatural union with a sea-maiden." Excusing himself, as we all love to do, he would add: "I did not, in fact, know that she was a maid of the sea. It is my misfortune that my steps are haunted and disturbed by the wild humours of her kindred, but it is not my crime."

By reflections like these, he felt himself in some measure strengthened; but, on the other hand, he felt the more ill-humour, almost dislike, towards Undine. He would look angrily at her, and the unhappy wife but too well understood his meaning. One day, grieved by this unkindness, as well as exhausted by her unremitted exertions to frustrate the artifices of Kuhleborn, she toward evening fell into a deep slumber, rocked and soothed by the gentle motion of the bark. But hardly had she closed her eyes, when every person in the boat, in whatever direction he might look, saw the head of a man, frightful beyond imagination: each head rose out of the waves, not like that of a person swimming, but quite perpendicular, as if firmly fastened to the watery mirror, and yet moving on with the bark. Every one wished to show to his companion what terrified himself, and each perceived the same expression of horror on the face of the other, only hands and eyes were directed to a different quarter, as if to

112

a point where the monster, half laughing and half threatening, rose opposite to each.

When, however, they wished to make one another understand the site, and all cried out, "Look, there!" "No, there!" the frightful heads all became visible to each, and the whole river around the boat swarmed with the most horrible faces. All raised a scream of terror at the sight, and Undine started from sleep. As she opened her eyes, the deformed visages disappeared. But Huldbrand was made furious by so many hideous visions. He would have burst out in wild imprecations, had not Undine with the meekest looks and gentlest tone of voice said—

"For God's sake, my husband, do not express displeasure against me here—we are on the water."

The knight was silent, and sat down absorbed in deep thought. Undine whispered in his ear, "Would it not be better, my love, to give up this foolish voyage, and return to Castle Ringstetten in peace?"

But Huldbrand murmured wrathfully: "So I must become a prisoner in my own castle, and not be allowed to breathe a moment but while the fountain is covered? Would to Heaven that your cursed kindred—"

Then Undine pressed her fair hand on his lips caressingly. He said no more; but in silence pondered on all that Undine had before said.

Bertalda, meanwhile, had given herself up to a crowd of thronging thoughts. Of Undine's origin she knew a good deal, but not the whole; and the terrible Kuhleborn especially remained to her an awful, an impenetrable mystery—never, indeed, had she once heard his name. Musing upon these wondrous things, she unclasped, without being fully conscious of what she was doing, a golden necklace, which Huldbrand, on one of the preceding days of their passage, had bought for her of a travelling trader; and she was now letting it float in sport just over the surface of the stream, while in her dreamy mood she enjoyed the bright reflection it threw on the water, so clear beneath the glow of evening. That instant a huge hand flashed suddenly up from the Danube, seized the necklace in its grasp, and vanished with it beneath the flood. Bertalda shrieked aloud, and a scornful laugh came pealing up from the depth of the river.

The knight could now restrain his wrath no longer. He started up, poured forth a torrent of reproaches, heaped curses upon all who interfered with his friends and troubled his life, and dared them all, water-spirits or mermaids, to come within the sweep of his sword.

Bertalda, meantime, wept for the loss of the ornament so very dear to her heart, and her tears were to Huldbrand as oil poured upon the flame of his fury; while Undine held her hand over the side of the boat, dipping it in the waves, softly murmuring to herself, and only at times interrupting her strange mysterious whisper to entreat her husband—

"Do not reprove me here, beloved; blame all others as you will, but not me. You know why!" And in truth, though he was trembling with excess of passion, he kept himself from any word directly against her.

She then brought up in her wet hand, which she had been holding under the waves, a coral necklace, of such exquisite beauty, such sparkling brilliancy, as dazzled the eyes of all who beheld it. "Take this," said she, holding it out kindly to Bertalda, "I have ordered it to be brought to make some amends for your loss; so do not grieve any more, poor child."

But the knight rushed between then, and snatching the beautiful ornament out of Undine's hand, hurled it back into the flood; and, mad with rage, exclaimed: "So, then, you have still a connection with them! In the name of all witches go and remain among them with your presents, you sorceress, and leave us human beings in peace!"

With fixed but streaming eyes, poor Undine gazed on him, her hand still stretched out, just as when she had so lovingly offered her brilliant gift to Bertalda. She then began to weep more and more, as if her heart would break, like an innocent tender child, cruelly aggrieved. At last, wearied out, she said: "Farewell, dearest, farewell. They shall do you no harm; only remain true, that I may have power to keep them from you. But I must go hence! go hence even in this early youth! Oh, woe, woe! what have you done! Oh, woe, woe!"

And she vanished over the side of the boat. Whether she plunged into the stream, or whether, like water melting into water, she flowed away with it, they knew not—her disappearance was like both and neither. But she was lost in the Danube, instantly and completely; only little waves were yet whispering and sobbing around the boat, and they could almost be heard to say, "Oh, woe, woe! Ah, remain true! Oh, woe!"

But Huldbrand, in a passion of burning tears, threw himself upon the deck of the bark; and a deep swoon soon wrapped the wretched man in a blessed forgetfulness of misery.

Shall we call it a good or an evil thing, that our mourning has no long duration? I mean that deep mourning which comes from the very well-springs of our being, which so becomes one with the lost objects of our love that we hardly realize their loss, while our grief devotes itself religiously to the honouring of their image until we reach that bourne which they have already reached!

Truly all good men observe in a degree this religious devotion; but yet it soon ceases to be that first deep grief. Other and new images throng in, until, to our sorrow, we experience the vanity of all earthly things. Therefore I must say: Alas, that our mourning should be of such short duration!

The lord of Ringstetten experienced this; but whether for his good, we shall discover in the sequel of this history. At first he could do nothing but weep—weep as bitterly as the poor gentle Undine had wept when he snatched out of her hand that brilliant ornament, with which she so kindly wished to make amends for Bertalda's loss. And then he stretched his hand out, as she had done, and wept again like her, with renewed violence.

He cherished a secret hope, that even the springs of life would at last become exhausted by weeping. And has not the like thought passed through the minds of many of us with a painful pleasure in times of sore affliction? Bertalda wept with him; and they lived together a long while at the castle of Ringstetten in undisturbed quiet, honouring the memory of Undine, and having almost wholly forgotten their former attachment. And therefore the good Undine, about this time, often visited Huldbrand's dreams: she soothed him with soft and affectionate caresses, and then went away again, weeping in silence; so that when he awoke, he sometimes knew not how his cheeks came to be so wet—whether it was caused by her tears, or only by his own.

But as time advanced, these visions became less frequent, and the sorrow of the knight less keen; still he might never, perhaps, have entertained any other wish than thus quietly to think of Undine, and to speak of her, had not the old fisherman arrived unexpectedly at the castle, and earnestly insisted on Bertalda's returning with him as his child. He had received information of Undine's disappearance; and he was not willing to allow Bertalda to continue longer at the castle with the widowed knight. "For," said he, "whether my daughter loves me or not is at present what I care not to know; but her good name is at stake: and where that is the case, nothing else may be thought of."

This resolution of the old fisherman, and the fearful solitude that, on Bertalda's departure, threatened to oppress the knight in every hall and passage of the deserted castle, brought to light what had disappeared in his sorrow for Undine,—I mean, his attachment to the fair Bertalda; and this he made known to her father.

The fisherman had many objections to make to the proposed marriage. The old man had loved Undine with exceeding tenderness, and it was doubtful to his mind that the mere disappearance of his beloved child could be properly viewed as her death. But were it even granted that her corpse were lying stiff and cold at the bottom of the Danube, or swept away by the current to the ocean, still Bertalda had had some share in her death; and it was unfitting for her to step into the place of the poor injured wife. The fisherman, however, had felt a strong regard also for the knight: this and the entreaties of his daughter, who had become much more gentle and respectful, as well as her tears for Undine, all exerted their influence, and he must at last have been forced to give up his opposition, for he remained at the castle without objection, and a messenger was sent off express to Father Heilmann, who in former and happier days had united Undine and Huldbrand, requesting him to come and perform the ceremony at the knight's second marriage.

Hardly had the holy man read through the letter from the lord of Ringstetten, ere he set out upon the journey and made much greater dispatch on his way to the castle than the messenger from it had made in reaching him. Whenever his breath failed him in his rapid progress, or his old limbs ached with fatigue, he would say to himself:

"Perhaps I shall be able to prevent a sin; then sink not, withered body, before I arrive at the end of my journey!" And with renewed vigour he pressed forward, hurrying on without rest or repose, until, late one evening, he entered the shady court-yard of the castle of Ringstetten.

The betrothed were sitting side by side under the trees, and the aged fisherman in a thoughtful mood sat near them. The moment they saw Father Heilmann, they rose with a spring of joy, and pressed round him with eager welcome. But he, in a few words, asked the bridegroom to return with him into the castle; and when Huldbrand stood mute with surprise, and delayed complying with his earnest request, the pious preacher said to him—

"I do not know why I should want to speak to you in private; what I have to say as much concerns Bertalda and the fisherman as yourself; and what we must at some time hear, it is best to hear as soon as possible. Are you, then, so very certain, Knight Huldbrand, that your first wife is actually dead? I can hardly

117

think it. I will say nothing, indeed, of the mysterious state in which she may be now existing; I know nothing of it with certainty. But that she was a most devoted and faithful wife is beyond all dispute. And for fourteen nights past, she has appeared to me in a dream, standing at my bedside wringing her tender hands in anguish, and sighing out, 'Ah, prevent him, dear father! I am still living! Ah, save his life! Ah, save his soul!'

"I did not understand what this vision of the night could mean, then came your messenger; and I have now hastened hither, not to unite, but, as I hope, to separate what ought not to be joined together. Leave her, Huldbrand! leave him, Bertalda! He still belongs to another; and do you not see on his pale cheek his grief for his lost wife? That is not the look of a bridegroom; and the spirit says to me, that 'if you do not leave him you will never be happy!'"

The three felt in their inmost hearts that Father Heilmann spoke the truth; but they would not believe it. Even the old fisherman was so infatuated, that he thought it could not be otherwise than as they had latterly settled amongst themselves. They all, therefore, with a determined and gloomy eagerness, struggled against the representations and warnings of the priest, until, shaking his head and oppressed with sorrow, he finally quitted the castle, not choosing to accept their offered shelter even for a single night, or indeed so much as to taste a morsel of the refreshment they brought him. Huldbrand persuaded himself, however, that the priest was a mere visionary; and sent at daybreak to a monk of the nearest monastery, who, without scruple, promised to perform the ceremony in a few days.

CHAPTER IX

It was between night and dawn of day that Huldbrand was lying on his couch, half waking and half sleeping. Whenever he attempted to compose himself to sleep, a terror came upon him and scared him, as if his slumbers were haunted with spectres. But he made an effort to rouse himself fully. He felt fanned as by the wings of a swan, and lulled as by the murmuring of waters, till in sweet confusion of the senses he sank back into his state of half-consciousness.

At last, however, he must have fallen perfectly asleep; for he seemed to be lifted up by wings of the swans, and to be wafted far away over land and sea, while their music swelled on his ear most sweetly. "The music of the swan! the song of the swan!" he could not but repeat to himself every moment; "is it not a sure foreboding of death?" Probably, however, it had yet another meaning. All at once he seemed to be hovering over the Mediterranean Sea. A swan sang melodiously in his ear, that this was the Mediterranean Sea. And while he was looking down upon the waves, they became transparent as crystal, so that he could see through them to the very bottom.

At this a thrill of delight shot through him, for he could see Undine where she was sitting beneath the clear crystal dome. It is true she was weeping very bitterly, and looked much sadder than in those happy days when they lived together at the castle of Ringstetten, both on their arrival and afterward, just before they set out upon their fatal passage down the Danube. The knight could not help thinking upon all this with deep emotion, but it did not appear that Undine was aware of his presence.

Kuhleborn had meanwhile approached her, and was about to reprove her for weeping, when she drew herself up, and looked

119

upon him with an air so majestic and commanding, that he almost shrank back.

"Although I now dwell here beneath the waters," said she, "yet I have brought my soul with me. And therefore I may weep, little as you can know what such tears are. They are blessed, as everything is blessed to one gifted with a true soul."

He shook his head incredulously; and after some thought, replied, "And yet, niece, you are subject to our laws, as a being of the same nature with ourselves; and should HE prove unfaithful to you and marry again, you are obliged to take away his life."

"He remains a widower to this very hour," replied Undine, "and I am still dear to his sorrowful heart."

"He is, however, betrothed," said Kuhleborn, with a laugh of scorn; "and let only a few days wear away, and then comes the priest with his nuptial blessing; and then you must go up to the death of the husband with two wives."

"I have not the power," returned Undine, with a smile. "I have sealed up the fountain securely against myself and all of my race."

"Still, should he leave his castle," said Kuhleborn, "or should he once allow the fountain to be uncovered, what then? for he thinks little enough of these things."

"For that very reason," said Undine, still smiling amid her tears, "for that very reason he is at this moment hovering in spirit over the Mediterranean Sea, and dreaming of the warning which our discourse gives him. I thoughtfully planned all this."

That instant, Kuhleborn, inflamed with rage, looked up at the knight, wrathfully threatened him, stamped on the ground, and then shot like an arrow beneath the waves. He seemed to swell in his fury to the size of a whale. Again the swans began to sing, to wave their wings and fly; the knight seemed to soar away over mountains and streams, and at last to alight at Castle Ringstetten, and to awake on his couch.

Upon his couch he actually did awake; and his attendant entering at the same moment, informed him that Father

Heilmann was still lingering in the neighbourhood; that he had the evening before met with him in the forest, where he was sheltering himself under a hut, which he had formed by interweaving the branches of trees, and covering them with moss and fine brushwood; and that to the question "What he was doing there, since he would not give the marriage blessing?" his answer was—

"There are many other blessings than those given at marriages; and though I did not come to officiate at the wedding, I may still officiate at a very different solemnity. All things have their seasons; we must be ready for them all. Besides, marrying and mourning are by no means so very unlike; as every one not wilfully blinded must know full well."

The knight made many bewildered reflections on these words and on his dream. But it is very difficult to give up a thing which we have once looked upon as certain; so all continued as had been arranged previously.

Should I relate to you how passed the marriage-feast at Castle Ringstetten, it would be as if you saw a heap of bright and pleasant things, but all overspread with a black mourning crape, through whose darkening veil their brilliancy would appear but a mockery of the nothingness of all earthly joys.

It was not that any spectral delusion disturbed the scene of festivity; for the castle, as we well know, had been secured against the mischief of water-spirits. But the knight, the fisherman, and all the guests were unable to banish the feeling that the chief personage of the feast was still wanting, and that this chief personage could be no other than the gentle and beloved Undine.

Whenever a door was heard to open, all eyes were involuntarily turned in that direction; and if it was nothing but the steward with new dishes, or the cupbearer with a supply of wine of higher flavour than the last, they again looked down in sadness and disappointment, while the flashes of wit and merriment which had been passing at times from one to another, were extinguished by tears of mournful remembrance.

The bride was the least thoughtful of the company, and therefore the most happy; but even to her it sometimes seemed strange that she should be sitting at the head of the table, wearing a green wreath and gold-embroidered robe, while Undine was lying a corpse, stiff and cold, at the bottom of the Danube, or carried out by the current into the ocean. For ever since her father had suggested something of this sort, his words were continually sounding in her ear; and this day, in particular, they would neither fade from her memory, nor yield to other thoughts.

Evening had scarcely arrived, when the company returned to their homes; not dismissed by the impatience of the bridegroom, as wedding parties are sometimes broken up, but constrained solely by heavy sadness and forebodings of evil. Bertalda retired with her maidens, and the knight with his attendants, to undress, but there was no gay laughing company of bridesmaids and bridesmen at this mournful festival.

Bertalda wished to awaken more cheerful thoughts; she ordered her maidens to spread before her a brilliant set of jewels, a present from Huldbrand, together with rich apparel and veils, that she might select from among them the brightest and most beautiful for her dress in the morning. The attendants rejoiced at this opportunity of pouring forth good wishes and promises of happiness to their young mistress, and failed not to extol the beauty of the bride with the most glowing eloquence. This went on for a long time, until Bertalda at last, looking in a mirror, said with a sigh—

"Ah, but do you not see plainly how freckled I am growing? Look here on the side of my neck."

They looked at the place, and found the freckles, indeed, as their fair mistress had said; but they called them mere beauty spots, the faintest touches of the sun, such as would only heighten the whiteness of her delicate complexion. Bertalda shook her head, and still viewed them as a blemish. "And I could remove them," she said at last, sighing. "But the castle fountain is covered, from which I formerly used to have that precious water, so purifying to the skin. Oh, had I this evening only a single flask of it!"

"Is that all?" cried an alert waiting-maid, laughing as she glided out of the apartment.

"She will not be so foolish," said Bertalda, well-pleased and surprised, "as to cause the stone cover of the fountain to be taken off this very evening?" That instant they heard the tread of men passing along the court-yard, and could see from the window where the officious maiden was leading them directly up to the fountain, and that they carried levers and other instruments on their shoulders.

"It is certainly my will," said Bertalda with a smile, "if it does not take them too long." And pleased with the thought, that a word from her was now sufficient to accomplish what had formerly been refused with a painful reproof, she looked down upon their operations in the bright moonlit castle-court.

The men raised the enormous stone with an effort; some one of the number indeed would occasionally sigh, when he recollected they were destroying the work of their former beloved mistress. Their labour, however, was much lighter than they had expected. It seemed as if some power from within the fountain itself aided them in raising the stone.

"It appears," said the workmen to one another in astonishment, "as if the confined water had become a springing fountain." And the stone rose more and more, and, almost without the assistance of the work-people, rolled slowly down upon the pavement with a hollow sound. But an appearance from the opening of the fountain filled them with awe, as it rose like a white column of water; at first they imagined it really to be a fountain, until they perceived the rising form to be a pale female, veiled in white. She wept bitterly, raised her hands above her head, wringing them sadly as with slow and solemn step she moved toward the castle. The servants shrank back, and fled from the spring, while the bride, pale and motionless with horror, stood with her maidens at the window. When the figure had now come close beneath their room, it looked up to them sobbing, and Bertalda thought she recognized through the veil the pale features of Undine. But the mourning form passed on, sad, reluctant, and lingering, as if going to the place of execution. Bertalda screamed to her maids to call the knight; not one of them dared to stir from her place; and even the bride herself became again mute, as if trembling at the sound of her own voice.

While they continued standing at the window, motionless as statues, the mysterious wanderer had entered the castle, ascended the well-known stairs, and traversed the well-known halls in silent tears. Alas, how different had she once passed through these rooms!

The knight had in the meantime dismissed his attendants. Half-undressed and in deep dejection, he was standing before a large mirror, a wax taper burned dimly beside him. At this moment some one tapped at his door very, very softly. Undine had formerly tapped in this way, when she was playing some of her endearing wiles.

"It is all an illusion!" said he to himself. "I must to my nuptial bed."

"You must indeed, but to a cold one!" he heard a voice, choked with sobs, repeat from without; and then he saw in the mirror, that the door of his room was slowly, slowly opened, and the white figure entered, and gently closed it behind her.

"They have opened the spring," said she in a low tone; "and now I am here, and you must die."

He felt, in his failing breath, that this must indeed be; but covering his eyes with his hands, he cried: "Do not in my death-hour, do not make me mad with terror. If that veil conceals hideous features, do not lift it! Take my life, but let me not see you."

"Alas!" replied the pale figure, "will you not then look upon me once more? I am as fair now as when you wooed me on the island!"

"Oh, if it indeed were so," sighed Huldbrand, "and that I might die by a kiss from you!"

"Most willingly, my own love," said she. She threw back her veil; heavenly fair shone forth her pure countenance. Trembling with love and the awe of approaching death, the knight leant towards her. She kissed him with a holy kiss; but she relaxed not her hold, pressing him more closely in her arms, and weeping as if she would weep away her soul. Tears rushed into the knight's eyes, while a thrill both of bliss and agony shot through his heart, until he at last expired, sinking softly back from her fair arms upon the pillow of his couch a corpse.

"I have wept him to death!" said she to some domestics, who met her in the ante-chamber; and passing through the terrified group, she went slowly out, and disappeared in the fountain.

CHAPTER X

Father Heilmann had returned to the castle as soon as the death of the lord of Ringstetten was made known in the neighbourhood; and he arrived at the very hour when the monk who had married the unfortunate couple was hurrying from the door, overcome with dismay and horror.

When Father Heilmann was informed of this, he replied, "It is all well; and now come the duties of my office, in which I have no need of an assistant."

He then began to console the bride, now a widow though with little benefit to her worldly and thoughtless spirit.

The old fisherman, on the other hand, though severely afflicted, was far more resigned to the fate of his son-in-law and daughter; and while Bertalda could not refrain from accusing Undine as a murderess and sorceress, the old man calmly said, "After all, it could not happen otherwise. I see nothing in it but the judgment of God; and no one's heart was more pierced by the death of Huldbrand than she who was obliged to work it, the poor forsaken Undine!"

He then assisted in arranging the funeral solemnities as suited the rank of the deceased. The knight was to be interred in the village church-yard, in whose consecrated ground were the graves of his ancestors; a place which they, as well as himself, had endowed with rich privileges and gifts. His shield and helmet lay upon his coffin, ready to be lowered with it into the grave, for Lord Huldbrand of Ringstetten had died the last of his race. The mourners began their sorrowful march, chanting their melancholy songs beneath the calm unclouded heaven; Father Heilmann preceded the procession, bearing a high crucifix, while the inconsolable Bertalda followed, supported by her

126

aged father.

Then they suddenly saw in the midst of the mourning females in the widow's train, a snow-white figure closely veiled, and wringing its hands in the wild vehemence of sorrow. Those next to whom it moved, seized with a secret dread, started back or on one side; and owing to their movements, the others, next to whom the white stranger now came, were terrified still more, so as to produce confusion in the funeral train. Some of the military escort ventured to address the figure, and attempt to remove it from the procession, but it seemed to vanish from under their hands, and yet was immediately seen advancing again, with slow and solemn step, among the followers of the body. At last, in consequence of the shrinking away of the attendants, it came close behind Bertalda. It now moved so slowly, that the widow was not aware of its presence, and it walked meekly and humbly behind her undisturbed.

This continued until they came to the church-yard, where the procession formed a circle round the open grave. Then it was that Bertalda perceived her unbidden companion, and, half in anger and half in terror, she commanded her to depart from the knight's place of final rest. But the veiled female, shaking her head with a gentle denial, raised her hands towards Bertalda in lowly supplication, by which she was greatly moved, and could not but remember with tears how Undine had shown such sweetness of spirit on the Danube when she held out to her the coral necklace.

Father Heilmann now motioned with his hand, and gave order for all to observe perfect stillness, that they might breathe a prayer of silent devotion over the body, upon which earth had already been thrown. Bertalda knelt without speaking; and all knelt, even the grave-diggers, who had now finished their work. But when they arose, the white stranger had disappeared. On the spot where she had knelt, a little spring, of silver brightness, was gushing out from the green turf, and it kept swelling and flowing onward with a low murmur, till it almost encircled the mound of the knight's grave; it then continued its course, and emptied itself into a calm lake, which lay by the side of the consecrated ground. Even to this day, the inhabitants of the village point out the spring; and hold fast the belief that it is the poor deserted Undine, who in this manner still fondly encircles her beloved in her arms.